# DO YOU REMEMBER
# THE BARN OWL?
## & other stories

# DO YOU REMEMBER THE BARN OWL?
## & other stories

### Written by
### Barbara Lorna Hudson

First Published in 2023 by Fantastic Books Publishing
Cover design by Gabi

ISBN (ebook): 978-1-914060-44-1
ISBN (paperback): 978-1-914060-43-4

# Acknowledgements

Thanks first and foremost to Dr Vera Baraniecka.

And thanks to other clever friends who have given me ideas for stories or helped me to improve them: Dr Lynette Bradley, James Brennan, Lindy Castell, Dr Keith Crook, Professor Nora Crook, Professor Alan Emery, Jan Gullachsen, Tomasz Klimek, Dr Mary McMenamin, Michael Pirie, Professor Michael McVaugh, Professor Geoffrey Walford. Also to fellow members of Writers at Blackwell's (led by Cherry Mostechar of The Oxford Editors) and of Oxford Writers Group.

And to my friendly, helpful publishers, Fantastic Books Publishing.

# Foreword

My foreword has been written at the insistence of a friend. She said, "As this is such a slim volume, a foreword might give your purchasers (if any) a bit more value for money." I thought this a rather cynical idea; but then I reflected that a foreword could help to explain a couple of things.

First question: why is it called "Do You Remember the Barn Owl? and Other Stories"? I have agonized about a title. It was originally "The Woman who Slept with a Monkey and Other Stories". Friends feared this could give a wrong impression.

"My Parrot died of Fright" was my next thought. That might intrigue potential readers, but it is a line from a story, not a story title, so I couldn't add "and Other Stories".

So I settled for the title of another of my stories that I hope is sufficiently intriguing.

Second: why produce an anthology when most of the contents have been published elsewhere? Yes, but many are in hard-to-access places, such as a blog and a defunct online-only publishing company. And it is a tidying-up exercise; most of the stories have been revised. It will give me an excuse for another launch party and I'll have a book to give people for Christmas. What's more: I don't feel properly published until my words are printed on paper.

It was Fantastic Books Publishing who suggested giving each story its own little biography. These may be of interest to anyone who wonders where plot ideas come from, and may encourage aspiring writers to just keep looking, listening and reading. Inspiration will come out of the blue as you go about your daily business and read the papers and chat with your friends. Sit agonising before a screen and it will elude you.

I hope you enjoy this book. And if you haven't already done so, do go on to write some stories of your own.

Barbara Lorna Hudson
Oxford, 2023

# What the Reviewers Say

Superb! Short stories but huge ideas. Acute, plangent, acidic and succulent. Imagine a cocktail of Roald Dahl and a very up to date, sassy, sexually liberated Jane Austen and you'll have something of the taste. Hudson's range is, well, everything: lust, ageing, loss, revenge, cruelty and redemptive kindness. Every tale has the frisson and directness of *haiku*.

Charles Foster, New York Times
Bestselling author of *Being a Beast*

I didn't intend to read the contents of this anthology in one go but Barbara Hudson's short stories were compellingly addictive so that's exactly what I did. There's a real mix in this excellent collection, from charming and poignant to the quirky and laugh-out-loud. Ms Hudson has real skill in creating atmosphere – she can whisk you from a hospital ward where a man is saying goodbye to his dying wife to the excitement of St Giles' Fair in Oxford. With tales of loneliness, revenge, a malevolent feline, and even a haunting, this author has it covered. I particularly enjoyed 'The Burning Bush'; it gave me a chuckle and fellow authors will understand why!

If you're looking for something to while away a couple of hours, I highly recommend this book; these stories will intrigue, shock, and make you smile.

Penny Hampson, author of *Writing History, Mystery, and a Touch of Romance*

Barbara Hudson is such a good writer and her dedication to her craft is astonishing.

**Rosie Millard OBE, journalist, writer & broadcaster**

Perceptive, sharp, poignant and funny, all of human nature and emotion will be found within this masterful collection of short stories every one a treasure to be savoured.

All of these short stories are original, entertaining , thoughtful and elegantly written, every word precise and resonant.

From the wonderful title story to the nostalgic and heart-warming 'Out of the sea' to the funny and sharp 'How Many Stars' they are treats to be treasured and re read.

**Carol McGrath, author of *The Handfasted Wife***

# Contents

# The Pimple

Helen is beautiful and wonderful and she has agreed to a date. Today is the day. If only George dared throw a sickie and have a lie-in. He needs to be well rested and look his best. Helen is what he has always dreamed of, and he doesn't want to blow it. He allows himself a minute or two of glorious sexual fantasy.

But first he'll have to struggle through a day at the office. He tumbles out of bed and staggers into the bathroom. There it is in the mirror, sneering back at him, not a trick of the light, not an aftershock from last night's nightmares—the first pimple of the year. The mother of all pimples. Big, juicy, in the centre of his chin, unmissable, undisguisable.

Should he cancel their date? No, he might not get another chance. Maybe the pimple will go down by evening. He dabs crossly at it with antiseptic cream, and the grease makes it even shinier. His hand hovers around it, but he controls his squeeze reflex. No, it will have to be a case of mind over matter and time heals all.

But time doesn't heal. His male colleagues tease him. Thank goodness they don't know about the date. The women seem to be avoiding both his eye and his chin. He tries to distract himself with work, but the computer screen blurs and all the emails and spreadsheets and documents and reports get overlaid with one gigantic, terrifying blow-up portrait of the pimple. He visits the loo so often that his colleagues ask if he is quite well. Each time, he glances around nervously to

1

make sure he's alone before examining his chin in the mirror. No change.

Helen's lovely face keeps filling his mind: her blue eyes, dark brows, high cheekbones, and the whole face a perfect heart shape framed with thick wavy hair. He can't visualise the rest of her but he knows she is not as tall as he is and she is curvy rather than plump or slim. His type exactly.

George wishes the time would drag, but it flies. Out of the distant past—his brief inglorious acting career in the sixth form—he suddenly recalls poor Dr Faustus, soon to go to hell:

Stand still, you ever moving spheres of heaven,
That time may cease, and midnight never come ...
The stars move still, time runs, the clock will strike.
The devil will come, and Faustus must be damned.

Comparing his predicament with Faustus' makes George feel a little better.

Back at the flat, he cleans the bathroom, bins old papers, gathers socks and pants off the floor, checks all surfaces for dust. He finishes the job with a blast of bluebell haze room freshener. Next, he puts his best white wine in the fridge and is pleased to discover some sophisticated spicy nuts to go with it. Just in case she can be persuaded to come back here. This thought leads to another burst of optimism and he changes the sheets.

Just in case ...

Then George takes a slow, thorough shower. He is desperately afraid that all this anxiety is bringing him out in a sweat.

"It's far too hot for May," he mutters crossly, "and all this blasted daylight will make it even easier for her to see the ghastly thing." He shaves gingerly around it.

What to wear? He tries a few variations on a theme, the theme being "smart casual", and settles for a plain blue shirt, a cream seersucker jacket, perfectly fitting blue trousers, slightly scuffed brown suede shoes and no tie. His thinning hair stubbornly refuses to provide cover for the bald spot which is shining in the heat, though not as fiercely as the pimple. He even remembers to clean his glasses.

The pimple hasn't changed. If anything, it has increased in size and hideousness.

Horrified, George realises he's going to be late. He rushes to The Golden Fleece. As he pushes his way through the crowded bar, he feels himself assaulted by the braying laughter of those happy, successful, handsome folk who frequent City pubs. Already he regrets suggesting this place.

Trembling slightly and half-tempted to do a runner, he looks for Helen. He only has her photograph on the dating site to go on.

They've agreed to carry the *Evening Star* as an aid to recognition. George has forgotten to bring one. He peers round in search of a woman on her own. There is only one such, at a small table in the shadows. She is gripping her handbag on her lap, a half-full glass of what looks like brandy before her, holding the *Evening Star* and reading intently. He can just make out the dark hair, the fine eyebrows.

He advances.

"Excuse me, are you Helen?"

She raises her beautiful blue eyes and starts to laugh so hard that her *Evening Star* shakes. Then she lowers the newspaper and smiles.

"George. How do you do?"

Her face is every bit as pretty as the photograph on the Internet. What's more, she has film-star teeth and just the right degree of curviness.

And in the middle of her chin—the cutest, the most endearing pimple. George grins broadly and holds out his hand.

The end

**The Pimple** was first published in *Click to Click: Tales of Internet Dating*, 2012. ed. Barbara Lorna Hudson. My very first attempt at a short story. I was doing internet dating at the time.

# The Easter Hamster

"You mustn't say he's dead!" shrieked Sasha, scarlet with rage, hands bunched into fists. "Miss Fisher told us miracles happen if we have faith. Father Hughes says the same."

Sasha's hamster had died, and he was only four years old, a year and a half younger than Sasha herself.

Clem looked at Shirley and spread his hands in a gesture of hopelessness. Shirley was the parent with the know-how, a social worker with a degree in psychology.

"We'll bury him in style, darling," said Shirley, "with a lovely ceremony to celebrate his life. Get some Christmas wrapping paper and that shoe box your new sandals came in. We'll make him a really beautiful coffin."

Clem was relieved. What a wonderful woman he'd married. He would never have thought of that. And, not for the first time, he wished he'd listened to her objections to sending Sasha to a faith school; this nonsense about miracles was only one of a series of pronouncements that Sasha had brought home since she'd started at St Bridget's. As devout Humanists, he and Shirley were at their wits' end trying to work out how to de-convert their daughter.

The ceremony went well. Standing at the graveside with Sasha and her parents were the neighbours' children and Mrs Scott, their cleaning lady. Sasha insisted on dressing up like Father Hughes with a white tea-towel for a dog collar and a black cloth wound round her waist for a robe. Having been to the funeral of a neighbour's dog, she had a garbled memory of what to say:

5

"Dear Sammy, we'll never forget your dust to dust ashes to ashes. Our father which art allowed be thy name ..."

"That'll do fine," whispered Clem. "Now throw some soil on the coffin." Clem was afraid of offending Mrs Scott, who he knew was a regular churchgoer.

The grave was shallow, dug hastily in the damp soil after an April shower. They laid a small stone on top, a pretty piece of quartz they'd found on the beach.

Sasha said, "He's got to have a headboard, too."

"Headstone. Good idea! We'll paint his name on a flat piece of wood," said Clem.

Sasha cried all evening. It was heart-rending. Her first experience of death. Shirley said it was right and proper to express your grief, and she encouraged it by bringing out photos of Sammy, and reminding Sasha of the day they brought him home from the pet shop.

Clem said, "Yes, and do you remember the day he pee'd on my hand and then bit my finger?" He laughed and then apologised.

But Shirley said, "That's OK. Nobody's perfect and we have to remember him as he really was."

Sasha cried some more and went to bed still sobbing. Clem was beginning to wonder if Shirley's approach really was effective.

It was Good Friday. Tomorrow the shops would re-open. He began to hatch a plan. He'd go out on his own and see what he could find. He chose not to tell Shirley in advance because he knew she'd try to dissuade him. He'd let her think he'd gone to buy Easter eggs.

He was in luck. The garden centre had a pet section and he found another hamster exactly the same size and colour as

Sammy. He bought two extra-large Easter eggs as well. When he got home, he found that Shirley and Sasha had gone to the supermarket. He took the new hamster to the shed and proceeded to transfer it to Sammy's old cage. When he picked it up—wishing heartily there was a tail to hang on to—the hamster whirled round and bit his finger hard. Clem screeched and let go. The hamster scuttled away, out of the shed, and across the garden, and disappeared under the hedge.

When Shirley and Sasha came in, Clem didn't mention the new hamster. If it turned up again, well and good. If it didn't … OK, best that Sasha didn't have to learn of this second disaster. He didn't dare tell Shirley; he knew he'd be in for a double-strength scolding, for buying a replacement so soon, before the grieving process was complete, and for carelessly losing that replacement.

Easter Sunday. Sasha went into the garden to pay her respects at Sammy's grave.

"Who moved the stone?" she demanded. The stone had rolled off the grave and the ground was disturbed. Clem wished to goodness he'd dug a bit deeper. There was a strong smell of fox and some claw marks in the soil. He poked gingerly at the shoe box. The Christmas paper was torn and the lid was half-off. And the corpse had vanished.

Shirley looked at him reproachfully. "Are you going to explain to her or must I?"

Different scenarios suggested, and then disqualified themselves. A much-needed dinner for hungry baby foxes? Too gruesome, though almost certainly true. A woodland re-burial with all Sammy's animal friends in attendance? Too fanciful, even for a five-year-old. Stolen by a fur-coat maker? No, that wouldn't do at all …

7

Shirley took over. "Now listen, Sasha. Sammy's dead. The real Sammy, the one we remember, isn't anywhere. You see, it's part of Nature's clever plan for a dead body to be of use to the rest of the world. To make the flowers grow. Or to feed the new little foxes or the baby badgers. You know how greedy those badgers are."

But Sasha wasn't listening. "It's a miracle," she said. "Just like Jesus. Sammy's risen."

"No, dear. That isn't possible."

Sasha rushed across the lawn to the edge of the border. She came back smiling broadly with a bedraggled golden hamster cupped in her hands. "Sammy's risen. Miss Fisher and Father Hughes will be so excited."

The end

**The Easter Hamster** was first published by Ether Books Ltd, 2012. A favourite with Humanist friends. The idea came from a news story about a seemingly dead hamster coming back to life.

# The Woman who slept with a Monkey

*Where do we come from and where are we going?* Our Quaker discussion group was never afraid to tackle the Big Questions. But taking on evolution *and* the life after death in a single two-hour session (including a comfort and coffee break) did seem over-ambitious, even to me.

Sitting next to me was a stout woman with faded red hair streaked with grey, at least ten years older than anyone else in the room. She seemed shy—overawed, no doubt, for we were an assertive, articulate lot, perhaps as a reaction to all the long silences during the Quaker meeting that preceded our discussion. After someone mentioned a recent wildlife documentary, the red-haired woman made a tentative contribution: "I once met David Attenborough. I had come to clean his office ..."

Everyone looked at her expectantly. She flushed. "At the time I'm afraid I didn't realise how important he was, but I'd seen him on the telly. And I knew he was a wildlife expert, so I asked him for some information. But he just said, 'Why don't you write to me?' and when I did, I'm afraid he didn't reply. I expect he was too busy."

Nobody troubled to enquire what she had asked David Attenborough about and I felt sorry for her because she obviously thought she had a big story and it had cost her a great deal to speak out.

The discussion continued and changed direction. What should be done with our bodies after death? Some favoured traditional burial; some urged 'green' burial in woodland; others wanted to be cremated and scattered about the place. There were even advocates of burial at sea and of exposure on a tower of silence to the ministrations of vultures. A few, like me, simply didn't care, but we joined in just as loudly as those who did care. My neighbour tried once to say something, but someone else talked over her.

"I'm Charles Barton," I said afterwards. "I think you're a new member?"

"I'm not really a member. I came because the topic interests me. Discussion groups aren't my thing—I either get tongue-tied or all muddled up. My name's Jenny Jones."

As she lived in my part of London, I offered her a lift. I wanted to make her feel a bit more welcome and, besides, I was a proud new driver, and the owner of a red second-hand Mini Cooper; at that age I enjoyed giving people lifts.

Away from the large group, Mrs Jones became more talkative. "Myself, I'd prefer to be cremated," she began. "But I do want a headstone. Will they let you have one just for ashes?"

"Oh, anybody can have a headstone," I replied, though I really didn't know. I was aiming for an academic career and in those days I thought one ought never to admit to ignorance. "Forgive my asking—why is a headstone important to you?"

"I've found a stonemason who could do a carving of an orang-utan for my headstone. I've priced it and everything and I want to put it in my will."

I jerked my head round. "Why a carving of an orang-utan?" She must be some kind of nutter.

"It's complicated."

"Please do tell me." I was hoping that at least she would provide me with a humorous story to tell my mates at college.

"I've had a thing about them pretty well all my life. I think it began with a monkey I slept with when I was young."

The Mini Cooper swerved. I wasn't used to such confidences from an older lady, especially on first acquaintance. I glanced at Mrs Jones. She looked deadly serious, and not at all embarrassed. She was dressed like my mother—discreet, old-fashioned skirt and jacket, sensible shoes. Nothing to suggest—well, what exactly? Surely not ...

"How do you mean—you slept with a monkey?" Only animal behaviourists out in the wild would have the opportunity for that. And then it would only be 'sleep' in the sense of 'take one's rest'. I took my eyes off the road and glanced at her again.

"Oh, it's not what you're thinking. Oh dear, I keep saying the wrong thing. I just mean I used to take my stuffed toy monkey to bed."

I was disappointed; not much of a story there. "And after you grew up?"

"I came across a photo of an orang-utan in a magazine and I sort of fell in love; he (I think it was a he) looked so very like my little stuffed Bimbo. I visit them at the Zoo whenever I can, and collect pictures of them. It's my dream to go and see them in the wild, but I'd have to win the lottery for that."

"Was it orang-utans you asked David Attenborough about?"

"Yes, how did you guess? I enquired if he had any contact with orang-utans. But immediately I'd posted my letter to him I realised I had expressed it badly. What I meant to say was, did he know any experts on orang-utans? Anyway, that came to nothing."

I tried to keep sarcasm out of my voice. "What a pity! You

must have been dreadfully disappointed." David Attenborough probably couldn't think how to respond, I thought. Poor man! he probably gets sack loads of loony letters every day.

"I don't really understand evolution," she went on. "But they say we're descended from the apes, don't they? And all this new stuff about genes and DNA—we didn't do it at school. Will scientists really be able to prove that people are fifty per cent the same as apes?"

"Or fifty per cent the same as bananas, or rhubarb," I replied in my superior 'I'm a science graduate' voice.

"Surely that can't be right? People don't look at all like bananas or rhubarb. And nor do apes."

Jenny turned away, and I realised I'd hurt her feelings. But before I could apologise or try to explain, she continued, speaking fast and sounding emotional. "I look into their eyes and they look into mine and I just *know* we're family. I believe I've got more of their DNA than other people. A sort of spiritual bond. I'm proud of it. I sometimes think they're better than us."

"But would they share their dinner with you?" This was my stock question when people got too anthropomorphic for my liking.

"Of course they would."

That was me told. Becoming impatient, I tried to take our conversation in a different direction. "Have you a family?"

"I'm divorced. I've two daughters, and three grandchildren. I adore them all, but I must admit I have a favourite: my daughter Coral's baby. Coral and Rufus have lived with me since the father ran off with a floozy he met in the King's Arms. Rufus is bright as a button, and so cute! Lovely auburn hair, a squashed little nose, and a big forehead like in that famous picture of William Shakespeare. He looks just like a baby orang-utan. Not Shakespeare—Rufus, I mean."

"Does Rufus' mother share your opinion of him?"

"Yes, in some ways, but she has no interest in orang-utans and I'm afraid she keeps calling the poor mite an ugly little b– . But I'm going to make sure he has the best of everything. I'm saving up for school fees. He'll be the first of our family to go to a private school and you never know—perhaps he'll get into Oxford or Cambridge. And if his mother doesn't love him enough, I'll always be there to make up for it."

We reached her street in a run-down council estate somewhere between Southwark and Greenwich, and I dropped her off. I waited till she was safely inside the block of graffiti-covered flats.

I never saw Jenny Jones again. The memory of that unusual conversation made me chuckle, and I enjoyed repeating it in the students' bar. I did not appreciate Jenny's devotion to the ill-favoured, fatherless baby, nor did I take seriously her ambitions for poor little Rufus; I felt these details made my story even funnier.

\* \* \*

That was forty years ago.

Although I've been a Green Party member for many years, I'm thinking of voting Labour in the General Election because I can't help admiring our Prime Minister. It's true, his looks are against him: his hair is a peculiar reddish-brown, and he has a large head, deep-set eyes, long arms and short legs. But what really matters is that he's concerned about poor people, single-parent families and animal welfare. He doesn't seem to mind being dubbed the Ugliest Prime Minister in Europe.

There's a photo of the Prime Minister on the front page of today's *Independent*. He's laying flowers at his beloved grandmother's grave. (Those insensitive paparazzi will follow him anywhere.) The headstone is in shot. Carved upon it is an orang-utan.

The end

**The Woman who slept with a Monkey**. Winner Plymouth Short Story Competition, 2019, this story was first published in *A Few of our Favourite Things Anthology*, 2019. It was inspired by a conversation with a woman whose main interest was orang-utans.

# St Piran's Well

The audience is down to five. It was fifty at the start of the university year.

Dr Martha Brown is punctual for her lecture, as she always is. And suitably dressed: navy skirt, plain white blouse and a string of pearls inherited from her mother. She doesn't get going till ten past twelve, hoping there'll be some latecomers; but there never are.

Try as she might—detailed hand-outs, apt illustrations, even a cautious sprinkling of jokes—she has failed to keep them interested. Their feedback forms tell a cruel story; it seems she lacks the certain something that her charismatic colleagues possess in spades. She fears there will have to be another little chat with her Head of Department—he'll insist she sign up for so-called teaching development seminars, or—worse —that he attend her lectures himself and mentor her.

The room is musty and small; out of kindness they have moved her from the big hall she was allocated in the first term. She looks despairingly at her audience. One of them has got the crossword out in readiness. She's aware they are only here out of sympathy. She wishes she knew how to reward and thank them for that.

She stumbles through the lecture. Here and there she stammers. Sometimes she loses her place in the notes and finds she's repeating herself. Not that anyone notices. Martha's faint voice grows fainter as the hour crawls by. When it's over—indeed, while she's still summing up—the young people begin stuffing their notebooks and tablets into their backpacks. "Have a good summer!" she says, and two of them reply, "And you!"

At last she makes her way out, eyes down, hoping she won't meet anyone she knows. She feels relieved; no more lectures till October. If only she could afford to resign this miserable job and quit this hateful city. She'd become an 'independent scholar' and write her book on the mediaeval sacred wells of Cornwall. She'd buy a smallholding and keep hens and goats, and become self-sufficient. Maybe she'd meet a kindred spirit to share her life …

She gets into the Micra. Drives out and round the Ring Road and on to the motorway. At the first service station, she pulls into the car park, opens the boot and hauls out a large battered suitcase. She carries it to the Ladies', feeling guilty— but surely *this* isn't illegal? She takes possession of the Disabled cubicle, feeling guilty again; hopes she won't make some unfortunate woman wait outside, desperate for a pee.

She takes out the dress. Cream silk, calf-length, floaty. And the transparent tights. And the cream shoes, almost too high to walk in. Then she changes. She packs away the skirt and blouse and the flatties.

Outside, she attracts some stares, but she forces herself not to mind and goes to the mirrors. Slowly, hands a little trembly, she applies makeup. Not something she's used to, for she only does this once a year, but she's had a practice run, and a professional lesson in Boots. "Less is more", she repeats the beautician's advice as she smooths on thin layers of lotions and lipstick and eye shadow.

Then it's back to the car and a steady drive to her

destination. She makes one last stop close to the entrance and lifts the hat gently from the round pink box on the passenger seat. It's a wide-brimmed, pink and cream creation, adorned with silk roses and long pale feathers. She puts it on and looks in the car mirror. Her bright red lips twitch with pleasure.

She drives smartly through the open gates. Unchallenged— the two officials don't notice that there's no car park badge on her windscreen. Then into Car Park No.1. She squeezes the little grey Micra between a maroon Rolls Royce and a silver Merc. Fortunately there's a big group just going in, chattering and laughing. The women are no more elegant than she is. She tags along as they approach the turnstiles. No one stops her. No one asks to see a ticket.

Martha enters the Royal Enclosure. Once inside, she keeps moving around, standing on the fringe of one group, then another, not wanting to look conspicuous. She clutches her designer handbag tightly. Inside is the folded betting slip.

The race begins.

"Come on, *St Piran's Well!*" she shouts, so loudly that her posh neighbours stare in disapproval.

### The end

**St Piran's Well** was first published in *Brilliant Flash Fiction*, Issue 8, 2016. I need to be discreet about the source of this one. NB the bad lecturer isn't me and I've never been to a race meeting.

# Lovely, Mr Shelley!

"Hail to thee, blithe spirit!
    Bird thou never wert …" On and on he droned.
    "Ooh, that was lovely, Mr Shelley!" said the young woman, when he came boringly to the end. "I adore skylarks!" she trilled.
    She was soft-soaping Percy Bysshe in the hope that he'd sweep her into his arms. He was said to be the greatest lover of the day, second only to Lord Byron. She wanted to find out for herself.
    Shelley began reciting again.
    By evening she thought she'd die of boredom.
    Mary could keep him.
    This settled the course of literary history.

The end

**Lovely, Mr Shelley!** was first published in *The Ball of the Future: Earlyworks Press Fiction Anthology*, 2016. I know some Shelley fans, and wanted to tease them (but they ignored it).

# The Counsellor

Michael sat bolt upright in the beribboned Rolls Royce, staring as if it came as a shock to find her beside him in a long white dress and veil. "Oh my god, Beth, was this really such a good idea?" Beth was learning a lot of psychology on her counselling course, but it hadn't prepared her for this.

Throughout the ceremony, her legs shook and she spoke in a low voice. But her bridegroom sounded happy and confident as he boomed out his marriage vows.

Now Beth took some slow breaths, willing herself to stay calm. She reached for his hand. "Oh, my dear. Think back. We went over it carefully before we decided. Can you tell me what's changed to make you feel different?"

"Hard to say. We're still the same people. This public commitment—it did seem right —it does seem right. But the finality—the feeling of no escape …"

"Michael, darling, I know the wedding makes it appear like that, but you're still a free man. It's not like going to prison for life."

"Not a life sentence. I suppose not. And you're not a gaoler." Michael laughed uncertainly and then relaxed back into his seat.

"OK. Now get ready to smile at our guests."

"Thank you, Beth. Thank you for being so understanding."

* * *

19

Two years later, Michael asked for a divorce. They agreed to stay in touch. Beth hoped he might change his mind. She found a flat and enrolled on an advanced counselling course. But the months went by and Michael didn't contact her except through his solicitor; Beth lacked the courage to make the first move. She worked at making herself more attractive. She chose her clothes with care, always wore makeup; she believed in being prepared, in case they should chance upon each other in the town. In fact, the first time they met again was at a party. Beth thought the host was hoping they might get back together. But Michael had brought a blonde who looked like a teenaged model. He left her, centre of attention in a group of students, and came over to Beth, who was standing by herself clutching her glass and a plate of untouched canapés.

"How are you?" Michael enquired. Then, not pausing for an answer, he began to recount everything that had gone wrong since they parted. His book got unfair reviews, a colleague stole his research idea, the washing machine flooded the kitchen. Beth listened, encouraging him to talk ("Tell me more"); empathised ("You must have been furious!") and reassured him ("Don't blame yourself— it could happen to anyone.")

Michael's companion interrupted them, winding her arms proprietorially round his neck. "Beth! How absolutely lovely to meet you!" she gushed. "Mikey's shown me heaps of photos and told me ever such a lot about you."

"This is Miranda," said Michael, beaming. He put one arm round Miranda's waist and to Beth's surprise, his other arm round hers. "I hope you two will be friends," he said.

The music started up loudly. Beth shouted, "Got to leave

now—early appointment tomorrow," and Michael shouted back, "I'll keep in touch, Beth!" while steering Miranda on to the dance floor.

Months passed and then they met by chance in the High Street. Michael invited her to a coffee shop. "Miranda and I have split up," he announced. He asked for her news and she began to tell him about her job as counsellor in a health centre, but he soon interrupted and went into detail about his own work: spats with colleagues and too much admin, and about his ill health: a bout of flu, an ear infection, an ankle sprained on the ski slopes.

He invited her to supper next day. She took a long time getting ready.

In the cobbled street she manoeuvred her Mini into a space behind the old Rover they'd once shared. She stayed in the car for a few minutes, renewing lipstick, running a comb through her hair; then sat looking up at the tall old house and across at the floodlit cathedral. At last, realising she was late, she got out and walked to the door, teetering on her new high heels. Her hand trembled as she pressed the bell. Michael welcomed her with a hug.

The kitchen-diner she'd planned, the curtains she'd made, even the wedding photograph on the mantelpiece—it was all as before. The only surprise was the lodger, Jamie, a young colleague of Michael's. Beth was introduced as "my ex-wife" and it felt terrible. Jamie said he had to go out, but Michael urged him to join them later.

Michael put on the familiar oven gloves shaped like fishes and with a flourish produced her favourite dish, his speciality mushroom lasagne. Beth did her best to eat enthusiastically. Soon he began to talk about his problems at work and his

21

growing suspicion that he'd taken the wrong career path. Beth listened and empathised. Before they'd finished their pudding Michael was sounding more optimistic, and was starting to work out possible goals and strategies to reach them.

After Jamie returned, the conversation became more general for a while, but reverted to Michael's disappointments and worries. Jamie turned to Beth. "He's been very low, you know. You seem to be doing him good."

"Yes," Michael agreed, patting Beth's hand. "She's a marvellous listener. I've been telling her all my troubles."

It was after midnight when Beth left for home. "Thanks for coming," said Michael.

Jamie stood apart while they hugged goodnight. Then he came forward and spoke to them both, "I can't work it out; you two just seem made for each other."

Michael looked down at the ground and Beth got quickly into her car. On a roundabout a lorry clipped her wing mirror and she felt tears running down her cheeks as she drove slowly back to her flat.

A week after this, Beth's telephone awoke her late at night. It was Miranda, the girl she'd met at the party.

"I expect you'll remember me," she said. "I couldn't think of anyone else to ring. Mikey always says you're the best person to go to with a problem, so I looked up your number. I'm in a bit of a state. No, actually, darling, I feel absolutely suicidal. Mikey's been blowing hot and cold for months, and now he seems to have dumped me for good. I can't understand it. What d'you think I've been doing wrong? D'you think it's his mother's influence? Silly old cow! And did you ever work out what it was he wanted from a woman?"

Bombarded with questions she couldn't deal with, and

astonished to hear from Miranda at all, Beth nevertheless listened sympathetically, providing no answers but letting Miranda pour out her woes. It was over an hour before Miranda thanked Beth effusively and rang off.

After several solicitors' letters, the divorce was finalised. Beth heard nothing more from Michael.

She eventually fell in love again. Beth felt she had no choice but to accommodate Christopher's desire to hang on to what he called his 'freedom'. A few days a week of 'quality time', he asserted, was better than getting under each other's feet. Beth used the evenings between their times together to give herself facials and paint her nails. "Like an old-style mistress," she joked. When he came to her flat, he would find the kitchen smelling of new-baked bread, a favourite dish in the oven and the best wine she could afford waiting in the fridge or on the table with the candles and flowers. The bedroom was redolent of Miss Chanel, the sheets freshly laundered.

After three years, Christopher ended their relationship. His "something to say to you" seemed to have been rehearsed. He waited till they'd eaten and then asked her to sit down in an armchair opposite him.

"It's me, not you. With your expertise you must have realised I'm commitment phobic. I've never managed to stay with anyone for more than three years. Something to do with my childhood, don't you think?" Beth was silent.

"You will keep in touch, won't you?" he continued. "I couldn't bear to lose your friendship. I've never been able to talk to anyone like I can talk to you." Beth still did not reply.

"Aren't you going to say anything?" He took her hand. "Please, Beth, I ..."

Beth wrenched her hand away and stood up. "Shut it!" she

yelled. "I'm not going to listen to your stupid explanations. And piss off! Now! I never want to see you again." Christopher called a taxi and left for the station laden with carrier bags stuffed with his toiletries and slippers and sweaters. She watched from the bedroom window as he went out of her life. Then she began to cry.

Next day, a John Lewis van delivered the largest bunch of roses Beth had ever seen. The card said "Sorry. XXX." She arranged the roses in a vase, but as their perfume began to fill the room, she took them outside and tossed them in the dustbin to join the remains of the *boeuf Bourguignon* and the empty wine bottle.

The telephone rang, but she didn't pick it up. She heard Christopher's voice recording a message: "Did you get my flowers? I wanted to say sorry and thank you for three wonderful years. I was hurt when you said "Shut it" and "Piss off"—so unlike you, Beth!—I thought you of all people would understand my feelings. I'm shell-shocked. I need to talk."

Beth pressed "DELETE".

The end

**The Counsellor** came from hearing of something similar happening to an empathic and door-mattish acquaintance.

# Satyr

The queues at the British Museum toilets were longer even than the one outside the Pompeii and Herculaneum Exhibition. The Exhibition hadn't opened yet, but the eager crowds were already gathering in the Museum and there were many desperate faces and crossed legs.

Lady Eldon had brought her son, the Hon. Jamie.

Lord Eldon had cried off. "I'm tired of culture," he said. This meant Lady E had a problem: at seven Jamie was a bit too old for her to take into the Ladies' and a bit too young to use the Gents' on his own. She scanned the men entering and chose one who looked both kind and harmless, a bit like Jamie's father, in fact: a man with a curly beard and an enormous belly.

"Will you keep an eye on my son? And make sure he washes his hands?" she asked, pushing Jamie forward. The man nodded, said something in an unfamiliar language, and led Jamie inside.

Later, in the Exhibition, Jamie halted in front of the Satyr Peeing. He stared at the grinning face and the huge belly, and then at the organ below, which was not really small, but was dwarfed by the overhanging blubber.

"Mummy! Guess what! I've seen that willy before!"

Lady Eldon was preoccupied with the sculpture of another satyr, this one making love to a very happy-looking nanny goat.

Jamie shouted again, "Mummy! I've seen that willy before!"

"Where, dear?"
"Where do you think? Doing a wee in the toilet, of course!"

The end

**Satyr** was first published in *The Ball of the Future: Earlyworks Press Fiction Anthology*, 2016. I got the idea after visiting the Pompeii Exhibition at the British Museum and queuing for the toilet there.

# Sandwiches for Seagulls

In a quaint Cornish cottage beside the sea, Emeritus Professor Gerald Cripps-Finkle is making dainty sandwiches. As he butters the thin-sliced bread, he sings a Tom Lehrer song from his youth, 'Poisoning Pigeons in the Park.' His wife Enid doesn't understand Tom Lehrer's black humour and clever political satire, so he plays the CD and sings the songs loudly just to upset her.

He thinks about the damp cucumber sandwiches and soggy asparagus rolls and sickly fairy cakes covered with hundreds-and-thousands that Enid inflicts on him when her horrible friends come to tea. Wizened old crones with clownish lipstick and hair dyed in strange, expensive colours. He reckons most of them are intellectually challenged. They have quite unfairly been permitted to outlive their far more deserving husbands.

He wishes he'd never agreed to leave his congenial university community to retire to this hovel that offers uninterrupted views of plastic rubbish all along the tideline, in a coastal backwater that reeks of rotting seaweed. The smarmy estate agent said it was a much sought-after location and when the Professor demurred, the agent convinced Enid by insisting that the place was free of low-bred locals: not a single Cornishman or Cornishwoman within miles, and full of genteel and cultured refugees from the south east, escaping its pollution and its hordes of unwashed undesirables. There would be queues of Professors, and Ladies This and That, and many a Sir Somebody or Other, all longing to make their acquaintance. Furthermore, there was a highbrow book group, and musical soirées within easy walking distance. The agent could guarantee they'd find it the perfect retirement residence for people like themselves.

Thereafter it was nag nag nag till the Professor finally gave in. He consoled himself with the thought that he could leave Enid in Cornwall for a good part of the year and return to his college, and go on enjoying the pleasures of laboratory, library and intelligent male conversation. But their savings have been hit by the recession; now he can't afford to travel back and forth and rent a college room. He's trapped.

The Professor has tried to improve the view by planting flowers alongside the wall of the tiny garden, but it's all ruined by the seagulls. They perch on the wall, bottoms directed inwards, and do their ghastly business. The noise they make is deafening. And the few times the Cripps-Finkles have ventured to take tea on the lawn, the gulls have snatched the food from their very hands; like the notorious seagulls of Padstow and Newquay, further down the coast, they'll soon be pecking people's heads as well as committing daylight robbery.

He's tried standing in the garden like a scarecrow, waving his arms about and shouting, throwing stones at them, spraying them with a hosepipe. Though he loathes pet animals, he borrowed a cat and then a dog —their names were "Fluffy" and "Toots" he recalls with distaste — but neither of the daft creatures paid any attention to the seagulls.

Feathered rats is what they are. But his silly, sentimental wife made a terrible fuss when he suggested rat poison: "No, Gerald, I won't hear of it. Rat poison is cruel. The poor things

28

can't help being seagulls. We mustn't make them suffer." He had to think up something more sophisticated. (Though he can't help wishing he dared give *her* rat poison.)

So now Professor Cripps-Finkle is making morphine sandwiches. He has ground up old pain-killer tablets and he sprinkles the powder evenly over the butter, puts the tops on, removes the crusts and divides the sandwiches into elegant triangles.

"What the hell are you doing, Gerald? I needed that bread for a summer pudding. Lady Geraldine's coming to dinner. As you well know. And what on earth do we want sandwiches for? If you think we're going for a picnic on a sweltering day like today, you've got another think coming."

She pushes him aside, grabs a sandwich, and takes a small, tentative bite. He hesitates but then shouts, "Stop! They're poisoned!" and she spits out the unchewed morsel.

"Honestly, Gerald, have you taken leave of your senses? You'd better come up with a good explanation for this piece of tomfoolery."

He explains his latest plan to get rid of the seagulls. She snorts, and calling over her shoulder, "Get rid of those sandwiches at once!" she goes into the garden and plonks her enormous bottom in the sturdier of their two deckchairs. Soon he hears a snore and a whistle through the open window. "God, what an unappealing woman!" he thinks.

He carries the sandwiches into the garden, tiptoeing past his sleeping wife, and lays them out in a neat row along the garden wall. Then he lowers himself carefully into the second deckchair and waits for his victims to fly in. He feels drowsy after a leaden Cornish pasty and three glasses of wine. The seagulls do not come and he begins to fall asleep. He dreams he sees a grimy, hairy hand sliding over the wall and seizing the sandwiches one by one, like those joke moneyboxes that snatch up coins from a little tray.

When the Professor and his wife awaken there are seagulls everywhere. The air is full of their screeches and screams. There are fresh droppings on the mesembrianthemums and aubretias, and the nasturtiums that Enid intended to put in tomorrow's salad. The seagulls seem perfectly healthy.

Yet all the sandwiches have vanished.

"Well, Professor Clever Clogs! Call yourself a scientist," sneers his wife, when he tells her. "So much for your cunning plan." Professor Cripps-Finkle wishes he had a gun; he'd be hard pushed to decide whom to shoot first, but it would probably have been Enid.

He rings up his old colleague, the Emeritus Professor of Pharmacology, and tells him about the sandwiches and their unusual filling.

"Heavens! Don't you neurologists know anything?" exclaims Professor Ferdinand Wisdom. "That would kill primates and people, but not birds. It won't have affected them at all. May I suggest you try giving your seagulls *Imodium*? You know—the stuff that stops diarrhoea.'

Next day, the Professor is looking forward to tackling the *Telegraph* crossword while his wife is at the hairdresser's, but the Vicar comes calling. A dapper, over-friendly man who seems to think they have things in common because they are both Cambridge graduates. As ever, he isn't welcome and he doesn't notice it. He walks in and appropriates the Professor's favourite leather armchair, oblivious to the newspaper on the arm and the half-drunk coffee on the table beside it. Exasperated, the Professor waits for the usual boring account of parish affairs. But today it's different: the Vicar brings news that makes the Professor jump.

"The old tramp, Jimmy, is dead. We missed him this morning; he usually calls in for a cup of tea and a sandwich. He was found over there, under the hydrangeas."

"Is there to be an inquest?" asks the Professor, trying to keep his voice steady.

"No, I don't think so. They know what he died of. He's been having treatment for a dickey heart, and the doctor saw him just yesterday, so there are no suspicious circumstances. Poor Jimmy—a harmless soul. A bit soft in the head, though. You know, he used to share his sandwiches with the seagulls."

"Well, well," thinks the Professor, relieved and amused. "This time Jimmy seems to have eaten all *their* sandwiches himself." He shakes his head and, concealing a smile, exclaims, "Oh dear, oh dear, poor old Jimmy!" 'Get Rid of the Tramp' can now be crossed off his list of things to do, though he hadn't intended it to happen this way; in fact, he'd forgotten all about the tramp, so intent was he on solving the seagull problem.

And there's still the biggest challenge of all: getting rid of Enid. Divorce or desertion would be time-consuming and expensive. Poisoning is out of the question, since they'd detect it easily and he'd be the prime suspect. Thoughts of rowing boat outings, cliff walks and dangerous kitchen appliances flit through his fertile professorial mind.

But one thing at a time. First, he'll deal with the seagulls. Gerald Cripps-Finkle doesn't give up easily. He didn't get to be a professor for nothing. He decides to demolish the garden wall and thus deprive the creatures of their perch. (Then there'd be a sheer drop at the end of the garden ...)

31

The end

**Sandwiches for Seagulls** was first published in Ether Books, 2012. It is based on conversations at an Oxford college.

# The Burning Bush

*The Burning Bush* (Vulture Press). An amateurish jacket covered completely with garish orange flames licking at a small fuzzy triangular object. It was not exactly clear, but the bookseller was sure this was a work of sado-pornography. Pink with embarrassment, "We don't sell this sort of thing," she told the author, a miserable-looking man with a peculiar moustache. "I believe this genre is only bought online. Or maybe in that 'Private' shop—not that I've ever been in there."

"Oh my goodness! Whatever did you think it was about? My dear young lady, this is an historical novel. Have you never heard of Moses' encounter on Mount Horeb?" He pulled aside his scarf to reveal a dog collar. The bookseller felt ashamed of her dirty mind. But she replied, "Would you come back when the bookshop manager is in? *She* decides about taking books direct from authors."

The manager glanced at the book. "Vulture Press? Never heard of them. It would be better if you got one of the Big Five publishers."

"Who knew?" muttered the author sarcastically.

"I beg your pardon?"

"Oh, nothing!" He marched out of the shop.

A week later he was back. The manager recognised him by his peculiar moustache. This time he sounded humbler. "Please could you reconsider stocking my novel? It has ten Amazon reviews now. I could do an event or a signing." He cast an envious glance at a celebrity author who was signing books for a queue of excited fans.

"We don't take self-published."

"It isn't self-published. It's from Vulture Press."

"Well, it *looks* self-published. Obviously print-on-demand."

He shuffled out looking stricken.

But after another week there he was again. The manager sighed. He was wearing down her resistance.

"I'll give it a week," she said. "Sale or return. If we haven't sold it by the weekend you'll have to take it away. Come back next Monday morning." She placed *The Burning Bush* in a dark corner where its lurid jacket was scarcely visible.

On Saturday night the shop with all its books went up in flames. Arson was suspected—there were signs of a break-in, and the police received reports of a person (gender uncertain) hurrying down the alley near the shop. The person wore a hoodie with just a white face showing, and there were no distinguishing features. He or she was carrying what might have been a book or might have been a handbag.

In sheltered accommodation for retired clergy some miles away, an author without a moustache smiled triumphantly as he watched the local news. Sitting by a cardboard box full of author's discount copies, with one slightly charred volume clutched lovingly to his bosom, he decided he'd lie low for a few weeks; then he'd look for a bookshop with a more discriminating manager.

The end

**The Burning Bush** was first published in *The Oxford Writer*, summer, 2018. It is a story fuelled by a longing for revenge.

# Dead in the Water

One Monday morning in June the tranquil life of Pete Higgins, the Upper Sudeley lock-keeper, was cruelly disrupted. His teenaged nephew Jason had come to stay, along with an enormous radio and a new-fangled iPod thing. While Pete had his breakfast he could hardly think—let alone read—for the crash and roar of rock music. That morning and the next two mornings he also heard a single loud bang and a splash, presumably part of the so-called concert.

On the fourth morning, Pete lost patience. "Turn that thing off," he yelled, on hearing again the bang and the splash. But his nephew had gone out leaving the radio on. Sighing, the lock-keeper put down the Parish Magazine and gazed out across the marigolds, geraniums and petunias in his prize-winning flower-beds.

Jason appeared a little later. He'd been for his daily jog down the towpath with a rock singer screaming into his ears from the iPod.

"Come and look! There's a dead goose in the river!" Jason shouted. The lock-keeper went outside. It was half-past seven on a lovely morning and the river sparkled. Floating near the lock was a blood-stained feathered shape. Some feathers were coming loose and the fresh blood was already disappearing in the water as the current began to carry the thing away. He wondered what had killed it. Well, he couldn't get near the carcass, and he didn't much care, so he returned to the Parish Magazine and his soggy cornflakes.

The bereaved relatives of the corpse were cackling and hissing and replenishing the carpet of stinking greenish sludge on the path. Last time anyone counted, the flock numbered thirty-one.

Their first meal of the day arrived with the Misses Jane and Belinda Fitzgerald, regular early morning walkers.

"Goosey, goosey, goosey," they cried, as they distributed their offerings of mouldy bread and half-eaten cake. Miss Belinda caught sight of the dead goose.

"Oh, the poor little thing!" She knocked loudly on the lock-keeper's door.

"There's a dead goose in the river," she said, when the lock-keeper peered out at them. "Whatever can have happened?"

"How would I know what it died of?" said the lock-keeper. "I can't reach the carcass and anyway, I'm not qualified to do an autopsy."

"What a shame!" said Jane. "Poor little thing never did anybody any harm. You know, they'll even take bread from your hand if you're patient and stand still."

Belinda started to speculate. "Maybe some cruel person shot it or wrung its neck. Could it have been poisoned? Or caught that virus from the swans?"

"Obviously shot—that's blood on it," said Jane.

"Any more missing? Let's count them."

The geese were crowding around demanding more breakfast, so this was an easy task.

"Twenty-seven. Four gone."

"The police should be informed."

"No, they've enough to do with all the burglaries."

"But if the killer used a gun ..."

"Those awful boys from the estate?"

36

Pete closed his door on the Misses Fitzgerald, still in full spate. But later, he began to feel uneasy. Perhaps those bangs he'd heard were gunfire? Ashamed of failing to take notice at the time, he phoned the local police.

"Some geese—they may have been shot ... No, I'm not exactly reporting an offence ... not exactly sure there *has* been an offence ... can't be certain the geese were actually shot ... No, I haven't got them here. I've only seen one, it's drifted downstream ... I don't mean to waste police time, but somebody said you'd want to investigate if a gun was involved."

"Oh, all right, sir. We'll look into the matter. We're a bit stretched at the moment." The officer was wary of this lock-keeper's tales —only last week he'd reported a body in the river and it turned out to be an old coat.

The news spread through Upper Sudeley. The Lavercombes were the first to be told. They were enjoying their muesli on the patio when Belinda Fitzgerald shouted over the wall. "Somebody's shot some poor geese by the lock."

Professor Lavercombe's reply was disappointing. "Delighted someone's trying to get rid of them at last. Do you know, we were just thinking of going into town for a new carpet. We keep getting their droppings on our shoes—the stains are impossible to remove."

Belinda and Jane hurried to the shop in search of a more sympathetic audience.

Meanwhile, in her quaint riverside cottage, Miss Marvell was enjoying the episode of *Midsomer Murders* she'd recorded the night before. After her morning walk she deserved a rest. She was quick to guess the identity of the *Midsomer* killer.

Then Miss Marvell went to the shop. She bought some nice

fresh spinach and some slightly rotten potatoes from Professor Lavercombe's allotment. The shop was unusually full because there was something new to discuss. Who killed the geese? And was it wrong?

As far as anyone knew, none of their circle owned a firearm, but everyone agreed that youths on the Honeysuckle Hill Estate might well possess airguns. Miss Marvell volunteered to check the gun licensing laws. Ever since she solved a previous village mystery, the case of the rude graffiti on the vicarage door, she'd commanded great respect. The people at last night's book club were impressed with her analysis of a P. D. James murder story, which further enhanced her reputation as an expert sleuth.

"Miss Marvell, don't you think it was the Honeysuckle Hill lads? We've seen them throwing litter, and I bet it's them that leave those syringe things under the hedge. It all fits together."

"No," said Miss Marvell. "I can't imagine *them* getting up so early. Anyway, the geese aren't exactly popular among our sort of people."

"They're a menace. The Budleigh-Hendersons' dear little grandson got pecked, you know. The poor child was trying to divide the bread up fairly, but they wouldn't wait."

"The mess is the worst thing."

"I'm sure whoever it was meant well."

The Fitzgerald sisters and their goose-loving friends joined in.

"We should find the culprit. We could report them to the RSPCA," said one.

"No, the RSPB," said his wife, who loved to contradict.

At the Residents' Association meeting 'how to get rid of the geese' was on the agenda again. No one could think of a legal solution. Miss Marvell offered to research the issue of Ruddy ducks and cormorants—harmless, attractive birds compared to geese, yet *they* were culled. Someone explained that Ruddy ducks mate with Spanish White-headed ducks and ruin their pedigree, and cormorants steal fish intended for the anglers.

The Vicar spoke movingly about how lonely people enjoy feeding their fellow creatures.

"In that case, they should get a dog," muttered Professor Lavercombe.

Over coffee, Miss Marvell moved around listening carefully. Clearly, the majority wanted the geese dead. However, no one approved the *manner* of the killing; they couldn't condone shooting in a public place. Indeed, if they identified the gunman, they'd feel duty-bound to inform the police. She concluded that the killer would be wise to say nothing.

One well-known resident was absent: the farmer, John Giles. John still grazed a few sheep, but most of his fields had gone for new housing. He had an Oxfordshire accent and vocabulary to match, a source of joy and fascination to his neighbours, who invited him to morning coffee, afternoon tea, and drinks and nibbles—but never to dinner parties. A token peasant for people wanting to prove their left-leaning credentials without having to mix with the rougher types from the estate, John was well-to-do because of his land sales, but he wasn't an educated man. He tried to compensate by attending evening classes and reading Dickens, but one humiliating evening at the book group had shown him how hopeless that was. He next tried to gain full acceptance by donating raffle prizes for the bazaar. In vain—he remained an outsider despite being the only real local in Upper Sudeley.

"So, Miss Marvell, what says our very own lady detective?" someone enquired.

"*One* person in Upper Sudeley might possess a gun. Farmers shoot rabbits and rats. Not that I've any proof, and I'm not naming names."

"Hmm … our friend John Giles isn't here. Haven't seen him with a gun, but he probably owns one."

"No reason to suppose he's lying low. He's gone to his granddaughter's wedding in Liverpool."

The killer didn't strike next morning and John didn't return till after midday. This lent support to Miss Marvell's delicate suggestion.

At the fete, people circled round John Giles. No one liked to ask directly, but they dropped hints.

"Must have been a gun owner. Not many round here."

"Would like to thank him personally for having a go."

"Wish we could. Decent fellow, whoever it was."

"I'd like to shake his hand. But he can't come forward – even with a gun licence, there's still that little problem about shooting in a public place."

"Someone in your line of work, eh, John?"

John Giles beamed and muttered something about not knowing, couldn't possibly say. He gracefully accepted a plate of fairy cakes from Professor Lavercombe, and noisy air kisses from several ladies.

Back home, Miss Marvell gazed at the portrait of the late Colonel Marvell of Killingdon Hall.

"Silly of me to throw your gun in the river, Daddy. I panicked when I heard a jogger rounding the bend. Now I can't kill any more geese. But I'm glad dear Mr Giles is getting the credit." She began scrubbing the greenish stains on her cream carpet.

The end

**Dead in the Water** was first published in *Oxtale Soup: stories of Oxford and Oxfordshire* ed. Sara Banerji, 2011. In a posh village near Oxford, not unlike my fictional Upper Sudeley, people object to the mess made by the local geese.

# The Sweetie

"I've waited seventy years for this." Jack Dawson punched Martin Gibbs in the face, shouting "Bastard! Thief! Paedophile!" They collapsed onto the ground, Gibbs with a bleeding nose, Jack clutching his dicky heart.

In court, Jack Dawson said, "Yes, I intended to hurt him. He deserved it."

Jack's lawyer said, "My client gets confused; he's deaf and he hadn't got his hearing aid in. He believed the victim said something rude about Mary-Ellen Smith, his care worker. He thought Mr Gibbs was interfering with her and had mentioned a roll in the hay—what Mr Gibbs actually said was 'Cold day!'"

\* \* \*

But now Jack's thoughts were elsewhere. He was back in the boys' playground at his village school.

It was wartime. Sweets were rationed. Jack had a single boiled one— a rich strawberry colour—in a twist of greaseproof paper. Mum said, "Keep it till after dinner," but he longed to unwrap it and have a nice suck. Ooh, the gorgeous flavour of strawberries and sugar—the lovely red stickiness. He'd roll it round his mouth, make it last.

Martin Gibbs gave him a hefty push from behind. Jack tumbled over, grabbed Martin's legs and pulled him down too. They wrestled. The precious little package dropped out of Jack's pocket. Martin grabbed it, unwrapped the sweetie and popped it into his mouth. A dollop of pink drool oozed onto his chin.

Throughout the next lesson, Martin kept turning round and poking out his bright red tongue.

"I'll get you for this," Jack muttered.

When Mum collected him, Jack pretended he'd enjoyed his sweetie.

Then came the holidays. Martin's family moved to another town.

\* \* \*

In their seventies, Jack and Martin met again; they were living in the same block of wardened flats. They had the same care worker, Mary-Ellen Smith. Jack kept forgetting her name, so he just called her 'Sweetie'.

The end

**The Sweetie**. Shortlisted Deddington Short Story Competition, 2014, this was inspired by a news story about one old man accused of assaulting another.

# The Civil War Walk

"I'd have cut off his head without a moment's hesitation. Had it coming to him. Sleazy, vain little git."

"Oh, Eric, I'm surprised at you. And what was so wonderful about your Lord Protector? A fine protector *he* turned out to be! Cromwell was a worse tyrant than King Charles."

"Fiona, you really must do some serious reading. You've softened your brain with too many bodice-rippers. Your grasp of history is pathetic."

"There you go again, always reminding me that I didn't get to university."

Fiona, Eric and Josie are in a flock of eager pensioners taking a Civil War tour of Oxford. Josie had been sitting behind Fiona and Eric on the Park and Ride bus. They were pointing and talking loudly as they travelled into the city centre.

"Remember that side road? We used to park the Morris along there."

"No we didn't, Fi. It was further out of town."

"I'd forgotten they'd built that enormous multi-storey!"

"Oxford's gone parking mad."

"The colleges don't like all the cars in the city centre."

"It's not the colleges, it's the Council. Honestly, Fi! If you read the paper you'd know that."

"That's the car park we sometimes used."

"No, dear. Not that one."

"Yes, Eric, that one. How could you forget?" They were raising their voices now, and Josie noticed Eric's neck had gone quite red.

Josie smiled to herself. Not a word about the beauties of Oxford, or even the shopping. Nothing but daft disputes about long-ago parking arrangements. Yet underneath the bickering she detected traces of a shared, happy past and a comfortable present: the way they touched each other as they pointed out of the window, the 'how could you forget?'

Josie felt a stab of envy, something that happened to her more and more when it ought to be less and less. Two years now she'd been on her own. Dumped unexpectedly after seven years —she still couldn't get it out of her mind. Retired, lonely, she was left to fill her time with activities like today's.

As they approached their bus stop, Josie heard Fiona and Eric mention the Civil War Walk and the Pensioners' Association, so she introduced herself, and they walked together to St John's College.

Sitting on the low wall, waiting for the tour to begin, Josie looks up and down the line of unfamiliar faces. Not one man without a partner. She's interested in the Civil War—of course she is—but she always hopes to get added value from these group outings, at the very least make a new friend. She decides to try to make friends with Fiona and Eric.

The pensioners struggle to recall their school history, some boastful about what they remember, others distressed at how much they've forgotten. People of this generation decided as schoolchildren which they'd have supported if they'd been alive in the 1640s: the Roundheads or the Cavaliers. Their guide tries to be fair to both sides.

They look up at the King and Queen, who gaze at each other across the Quad in St John's College. Despite centuries of student pranks—statue abuse—the bronze statues gleam in the sunlight as if they'd been erected yesterday.

"They were deeply in love," says the guide, a catch in his voice, "though poor Henrietta Maria was unhappy when she first came to England."

They look a handsome couple and the guide does not mention that the King was very short and afflicted with a stammer and the Queen had sticking-out teeth. Charles was a faithful husband who adored his Queen, and their time together was cruelly curtailed. These statues were put up before the Civil War, and it was as though the builders of this quadrangle, placing them apart rather than side by side, foresaw their tragic future.

As the tour continues on through the city, the guide tries to right the balance. He talks of the appalling behaviour of the King's troops, who took up residence when the Court moved to Oxford. The violence, extortion, protection rackets.

The Colleges were forced to hand over their gold and silver plate to be melted down. The only exemptions were for pieces used in the Communion service. Some Colleges pretended that *all* their plate was Communion plate; others hid it away. St John's College offered £800 instead; the King graciously accepted the money and then took the plate as well.

Eric smiles at his wife's discomfiture. "So your Royalists weren't such a saintly bunch, were they?"

Josie observes that the Roundheads weren't in Oxford at the time, so it isn't surprising that these offences were all committed by Royalists. Fiona ignores her, and Eric looks at her sharply but doesn't respond. She realises it's his wife he wants to argue with, not her.

In any case, Eric's triumph doesn't last long. They come to the Church of St Mary. Its unusual Baroque porch caught the eye of a Roundhead soldier marching into the town after it fell to the Parliamentary army. He shot the heads off the Virgin and Child.

Fiona and Eric go on arguing about royalism, religion and the misdeeds of the two sides. Josie's attempts to participate are met with little more than an occasional polite nod, so she resigns herself to simply listening in. Fiona and Eric's argument escalates into a quarrel.

Don't they appreciate what they've got?

What Charles and Henrietta Maria had, too. The royal couple celebrated their reunion after the Battle of Edgehill with a special coin. They spent most afternoons together at the Queen's rooms in Merton College, the King coming to her out of Christ Church via the back gateway cut through especially for him. He rode at her side all the way to Abingdon, where they parted for the last time; when they said goodbye, she fainted.

Josie is surprised at herself, and ashamed. How could she envy a long-dead, beheaded king and the sorrowing queen he left behind? Or the bickering elderly couple in front of her? Answer: she envies them the lasting partnership she has never achieved.

The tour ends and the guide recommends a nearby teashop. Fiona and Eric turn to Josie. "Goodbye. Nice to have met you," says Eric, and he takes his wife's arm. "Come along, Fi, I'm going to buy you an enormous piece of chocolate cake," and they walk off.

As Josie comes out of the Meadows into the War Memorial Garden, she suddenly sees a once-familiar, much-loved figure. Unmistakeable posture as he strides along: chin slightly forward as though keen to get to what life has next to offer; same old black jacket slung over one shoulder. Within touching distance. Laughing. Hand-in-hand with a tall, grey-haired woman.

Did he see her? Hard to tell. When she met him by chance last year, that encounter hit her like a second loss. This time she walks on by, but then she stops and turns to watch him going away. He doesn't look round. She tells herself that seeing him hasn't changed anything. She's no more alone now than she was yesterday.

The end

**The Civil War Walk** was first published in *Oxtale Soup: stories of Oxford and Oxfordshire*, ed. Sara Banerji, *2011*. It was written after a walking tour of Civil War Oxford.

# Dr Dodgson and Mary Jane

"Ooh, Dr Dodgson, the boat's leaking."

They were rowing up the Thames on their way to the Treacle Well.

"Sit still Mary Jane, or we'll—"

Down they went. In the mud at the river bottom, Mary Jane met the White Rabbit. Then all went black. Charles Dodgson swam to the bank. He'd have to find another little girl; he needed one for inspiration if he was ever going to finish *Alice in Wonderland*.

The end

**Dr Dodgson and Mary Jane** was first published in *The Ball of the Future: Earlyworks Press Fiction Anthology*, 2016. It was written in my house overlooking the Thames in Oxford.

# The Seal and the Cavalier

There's a life-size stone seal in the garden pond. A pair of mallards are waddling across the lawn. A red kite is circling overhead, but the old man peering out through the murky window pays no attention to the kite.

Colin Bolton retired from the bank fifteen years ago and exchanged the tyranny of his workplace for the tyranny of his wife Betty. They ended up here: a two-bed bungalow in a nondescript village. But it's near a couple of shops, a bus stop, and a pub, and it has parking for two cars. The Morris Minor is rusting in the garage, for Colin can't drive any more.

They bought the place because their daughter Tamsin lives nearby. Betty insisted, although Colin had dreamed of retiring to the seaside. His service in the Navy was the happiest time of his life, that and their honeymoon in Cornwall. This village couldn't be further from the sea.

The seal helped to swing it —worth a few hundred pounds, according to the estate agent. Betty said, "It's an ugly thing, but we can always sell it if we need a bit extra," and he said, "Please, dear, I'd like to keep it—something to remind me of the sea."

Everyone says you should take up a hobby when you retire. Betty didn't want one. But she allowed Colin to join the local history society. He'd always loved history, and at school he'd enjoyed that debate every Englishman over fifty remembers: which side would *you* have supported in the English Civil War—Cavalier or Roundhead?—King or Parliament? Colin would have been for Parliament, a Roundhead, fighting for freedom against the tyrant King Charles.

It all came back to him when he went to see Chalgrove Field, a few miles from their new home. The Battle of Chalgrove, 1643: the local MP, John Hampden, led a regiment of the Parliamentary Army, lost to Prince Rupert's troops, and was fatally wounded there. Even before this, John Hampden was a hero, known as 'The Patriot' or 'Father of the Nation' because of his brave stand against the King's illegal taxes.

Colin joined the Sealed Knot, the society that re-enacts Civil War battles. Well into his seventies, he still dressed up as a Parliamentary soldier and ran about and shouted and fired his musket.

But arthritis and emphysema have put a stop to all that. He can't even get to their indoor meetings now.

Betty is dead and he wishes he was somewhere else. Today he's awaiting one of his daughter's rare visits, with her greedy husband Geoff and their two sullen teenagers.

As the Range Rover squeezes into the driveway, Colin notes with relief that his grandsons have stayed away. Tamsin gives him an air kiss—a new habit of hers. He wonders if it is to protect her pancake makeup, which is almost exactly the same colour as her posh camel hair coat. He's puzzled to see Geoff unload a large framed print, Frans Hals' *Laughing Cavalier*. Colin recognises it dimly—it used to hang in the hall of Geoff and Tamsin's previous house before they went upmarket and did a de-clutter.

Tamsin says, "We want to do a swap. Give us that seal from the pond and you can have this lovely picture in exchange. You know you love those old Cavaliers and Roundheads. Well, here's a nice friendly Cavalier for you."

"But, I ..." He'd like to explain that he's doesn't love the Cavaliers. And, what's more, *this* so-called Cavalier isn't a member of the King's army in the English Civil War. He isn't even a soldier. Nor even the same period—twenty years earlier, and in Holland, not England.

"Honestly, Colin, the seal looks absurd in your tiny little pond. It'll fit in far better in ours—ours is more like a small lake, really." That loud, condescending voice his son-in-law has used on Colin since Colin's seventieth birthday.

"Pretty please, Dad. Geoff's set his heart on it." Tamsin puts on the little-girl smile that has always won him round. As controlling as her mother, he thinks, though her strategies are different.

He would like to tell them about his honeymoon in Cornwall and the seals he and Betty saw there, but he knows they wouldn't be interested. He agrees to the swop.

While Colin is making tea in the kitchen, he overhears their conversation.

"Oh my God, Geoff. See what I've found—this is a brochure for an old people's home. In Cornwall, of all godforsaken places!"

"Look at the fees! Your dad's savings would be swallowed up in no time. And the proceeds from this bungalow, too."

"Geoff, we've got to stop him. When he dies there'd be nothing left for us. And I bet he'd linger on in the lap of luxury for years, just to spite us."

"We'll have to persuade him to change his mind. No point in reasoning with him, though, he's a stubborn old git. Now your mum's gone he thinks he can do what he likes. I'm afraid we're going to have to trek over here more often and do a few little jobs for him, make him want to stay put."

* * *

After the visit is over, Colin hangs the *Laughing Cavalier* in his bedroom; then he moves it to a dark corner of the lounge. He hates the man's smirk—anyone can see it isn't a laugh— and that silly hat and improbable moustache and ostentatious outfit. Worst of all, *The Laughing Cavalier* is one of those portraits with eyes that follow you around the room and you wish they wouldn't.

Next day, he carries the picture outside and tosses it face down into the pond. The glass cracks as it hits the stone seal. A moment later, taking pity on the goldfish, he hauls it out again, and sneaks it into a builder's skip halfway down the road.

Geoff and Tamsin send a couple of workmen, who after a lot of cursing and hacking manage to prize the seal off its cement base. They hoist it on to their pick-up truck and drive away.

Colin gets a taxi to Chalgrove Field. Leaning on his stick, he looks up at the John Hampden monument. "Time to say goodbye, my friend."

Back at the bungalow, he picks up the brochure and dials a number. He asks if there are any vacancies at the Seaview Retirement Home near Newquay, Cornwall.

The end

**The Seal and the Cavalier** was written after a visit to Chalgrove Field, site of a Civil War battle.

# Potter, Dimity, Lilies

I'm on my own now, a sad old lady rattling around in the big haunted Rectory. The old ghost doesn't bother me; but I'm grieving for Jack. I miss him so much, and sometimes I think I hear his voice. And sometimes, out of the corner of my eye, I think I glimpse a little pale pink emanation floating by. Could Jack, too, have become a ghost? The Church would say it's impossible, because Jack didn't have a soul.

Jack and I grew old together. I began as a brunette and went grey. Jack began grey and went pink: African Greys do that.

Some people have geese instead of a watchdog, but you have to keep them in your garden and they make an awful mess. And they're terribly noisy, even when there aren't any intruders. My parrot, Jack, was as alert as a burglar alarm. And more loving than any dog.

Jack and I moved into the Old Rectory after Uncle Jim died and left it to me. Too big for one person, but I was delighted to leave my boxy little flat. I'd been a history teacher and I'd always dreamed of having a piece of history of my own.

The Rectory: an ancient, spooky house crying out for dastardly deeds. I'd spent summer holidays here as a child; but it wasn't until I was fifteen that Uncle Jim told me the story of the priest.

"It was the time of Henry VIII's Reformation," said Uncle Jim. "The priest refused to abandon the traditions of the Catholic Church. When Thomas Cromwell's thugs came calling, he resisted arrest and tried to reason with them. One of them flew into a rage, drew his sword and pierced the priest through the heart. Just outside the front door, it was. At the very moment of death, the saintly man forgave his killer, who was so moved and ashamed that he threw away his sword and left Cromwell's service. The story has come down through the generations in the village.

"There have been the occasional sightings of an entity hovering about in the garden, a sort of black floating thing with a white face and staring eyes. And some people passing the house on an autumn night claim to have seen … well, a sort of film clip of the dying priest falling to his knees, with the sword blade entering his breast as he falls."

I must have looked alarmed, for Uncle Jim added, "Don't you worry, Mary, my dear. It's never been seen during the school holidays." And I don't remember the subject coming up again.

\* \* \*

By the time I came to live in the Rectory, I no longer believed in ghosts, and after I'd got the brambles and the ivy cleared, it didn't seem so creepy.

However, on my third night, I heard noises in the garden. Jack squawked and there were running footsteps along the gravel path and the sound of the iron gate clanging shut.

The Police advised double glazing and window locks.

"You're a bit isolated here," they said, stating the obvious. "Just you and the parrot."

I took their advice. But I wasn't overly worried. The house looked shabby, the great door in need of painting, the gutterings hanging loose, old broken tiles on the roof, and with my little Morris Minor parked outside, any passing villain would realise there was nothing worth stealing.

Next, I decided to redecorate. People in the village recommended Paolo Rossi. Italian by birth, he'd lived in the district for many years, but ended up in a hostel in town after his English wife ran off with his savings and his workmate. Now Paolo was looking for a job with accommodation, and his references stressed his skill and reliability.

I interviewed Paolo. He'd come here from Sicily. He was very polite and soft-spoken until he began to talk about his wife's desertion. "She has dishonoured me," he shouted, making me start. "When I catch that no-good Peter Watson, I cut him into little, little pieces and I make my wife blue and black." Fortunately for them, Paolo had not been able to locate the couple.

Paolo came to live in the rooms downstairs. I felt a bit safer with him on the premises.

On October 10th, six months after I had moved into the Rectory, Paolo was nowhere to be found. All his possessions had gone, and there was no note and no bill, though I owed him for a week's work.

That day, I heard Jack repeating some new words: three words in a foreign language. Italian? Spanish? Or was it English, after all? It sounded like 'Potter, dimity, lilies' and he followed them with a heart-rending moan. Had someone been reading Harry Potter to Jack? But who? Jack had come to live with me long before the first Harry Potter book was published, and I'm not a fan. Anyway, I doubted if those books mentioned dimity or lilies. No, I decided, the three words definitely weren't English.

I called the police because I was worried about Paolo. Had someone done something awful to him? Had he reverted to his native Italian in his agony, then moanedand possibly died, with poor Jack the only witness to the crime?

"But did you hear anything?" the police sergeant enquired.

"No," I said. "I like a sup of whisky as a nightcap, and I take my hearing aid out at bedtime."

I begged the police to listen to Jack. They were sceptical. "It's hardly likely a parrot could repeat something after hearing it only once."

"Oh yes, Jack could," I insisted. "This is an exceptionally gifted parrot."

The words certainly sounded like Italian, but the police refused to call in an interpreter. "Those people charge an arm and a leg," they said.

I was unable to persuade them that Jack might hold the key to Paolo's sudden disappearance.

The police pointed out there were no signs of a break-in; no blood; no evidence of struggle; no fingerprints, except my own and Paolo's. Nothing of mine had been taken—not my purse, not my treasured silver candlesticks—indeed, Paolo had left me in his debt. I liked him, and I'd been right to trust him, for he was obviously no thief. Even his door key had been put back on its hook in the hall.

The following week, Paolo was arrested. He'd traced his wife and Peter Watson to a small town not five miles away. The police caught him on the run after a botched attempt at stabbing Watson with a blunt kitchen knife. He wrote me a sad letter from gaol, apologising for his moonlight flit. "That night I couldn't sleep. Kept imagining I heard noises. I wasn't thinking straight. I'd found out where my wife and that bad man had gone and I made a sudden decision to go after them. I didn't want to involve you, so I left while it was still dark."

Jack continued the strange utterances and the awful moans.

\* \* \*

My university friend, Alastair Foster, came to stay. Besides being a dab hand with a paintbrush, he happens to be a professor of Tudor history. He listened to Jack for a while and when Jack spoke the mystery words, Alastair said, "Sounds like Latin, but I can't understand it."

"How can it be Latin? Nobody speaks Latin."

"Only a few people in the Vatican ..." Alastair was a stickler for absolute accuracy. He continued, mystified, "I can't make this out at all. Maybe your parrot has invented a new language of his own."

When he'd finished the decorating that poor Paolo had begun, Alastair set about some research. He spent a day in Oxford and found a sheaf of sixteenth-century records at the Oxford college that owned the living. "Yes, a priest who lived here was murdered. On the night of October 9th, 1539, to be exact. Probably preferable to the fate they had in store if he'd been taken alive."

Alastair helped me in the garden, too. One day, he was digging out a flower bed while Jack looked on from his perch outside the door. I stood beside the perch, feeding Jack bits of pineapple and telling him for the umpteenth time what a pretty boy he was. Suddenly there came a shout from Alastair: "Mary, look at this! This is amazing!" and immediately after, Jack let out a shriek of alarm.

Alastair was advancing towards Jack and me, brandishing an object he'd pulled out of the soil. A long, tapered blade with a handsomely shaped hilt. A rusty, muddy old thing, but unmistakeable: a sword, a Tudor sword.

"*Pater dimitte illis*," said Jack clearly. Then he moaned and dropped off his perch.

"Father forgive them," Alastair translated, while I attempted mouth-to-beak resuscitation.

The vet concluded that my parrot had died of fright.

The end

**Potter, Dimity, Lilies.** Runner-up, Spooky Tales Competition, this was first published in *What the Dickens? Spooky Tales Collection,* 2014. A woman I met claimed her parrot could learn a new phrase after hearing it only once.

# The Grave Robbers

Arthur Fletcher squared his shoulders and strode along the ward, walking like the soldier he'd once been. He was wearing his best tweed jacket and the blue tie Beryl bought him last Christmas; he wanted to look smart for her. His wife smiled as she watched from her bed at the far end of the ward. He could hardly make her out for all the wires and tubes, and she looked tiny; even the narrow hospital bed seemed far too big for her. The image of the coffin at his brother's funeral came into his mind; how small we can look when we come to the end.

"I couldn't bring you any flowers, my dear. The garden's bare."

"Well, we never were ones for shop-bought flowers and suchlike," Beryl said in her quiet voice.

"I never could afford to treat you like a lady."

"But Arthur, you always did treat me like a lady." There was a short silence, broken only by the rhythmic hiss of the machines. Then Beryl said, "I suppose they'll have reduced my pension, now I've been in hospital so long?"

"Yes, they have."

"But the bills don't stop, do they? I hope you're keeping warm? No cutting back on the heating?"

"Don't you worry about me. Just concentrate on getting better and coming home."

"Arthur, dear, I don't think I'll be coming home."

They fell silent and he squeezed her hand.

"I'm not afraid, Arthur. I just hope you'll be all right."

"I'll be all right, Beryl."

Later, as he was leaving, the ward sister asked him to come into her office.

"Mr Fletcher, how do you find your wife?"

"Not good, nurse. She doesn't look good at all."

"That's why I need to talk to you. She isn't in any pain, and she won't be, I can promise you that. But we're afraid this time she's not going to pull through."

"How long?"

"A few days at most."

"I see." He stood up quickly, steadied himself on the chair, said a brisk goodbye and left before the nurse could stop him. It was the thirteenth of February. Never once had he given her flowers on Valentine's Day; this was his last chance. Back home, he looked in his wallet and the jar where they kept spare cash. But there was only enough for a card.

Though he didn't feel hungry he made some toast and bit into it angrily. Then he recalled his brother's burial and the flowers on the graves in the churchyard. He put on his coat and hat, picked up his torch and walked down the road to St Crispin's.

Rain was falling and clouds kept covering the moon as he made his way along the gravel paths, swinging the torch beam from side to side on to the graves. At last he found a grave with flowers on it. A bunch of pink carnations. He stopped and shone his light on to the black marble headstone: *Beryl Rhodes, beloved wife of Charles and mother of Christine and Jennifer. Aged Forty Years.*

He'd never stolen anything in his life. Would this other Beryl forgive him? Would Charles and Christine and

Jennifer? No, they'd react with horror: they'd think he was just a heartless petty thief. And what would his own Beryl say if she knew? He hesitated, and feeling shaky, sat down heavily on a bench.

Then he pictured his Beryl's face on receiving her first Valentine's flowers. She need never know where he'd got the carnations and the person who brought them here wouldn't know they'd been taken. The lady in the grave—well, she was dead and gone; she no longer needed flowers.

Arthur stood up and was approaching the grave when he heard hurried footsteps crunching down the path.

He moved sideways behind a large yew tree.

A young girl came into view, looking nervously around her, her thin jacket and jeans drenched and her blond hair flattened by the rain. She headed for the grave and grabbed the flowers. He could hear her sobbing as she stowed them carefully into a plastic carrier bag. She looked up and caught sight of him.

"Oh, please, don't shop me. I'll put them back."

He came out from behind the tree. "You and I are as bad as each other. I was going to do what you've just done."

"I'm sleeping rough. Sick of begging. I know this is sort of stealing, but the woman's dead after all, so what use are they to her? I can sell them outside the pub—mean old gits want to give their wives flowers but don't want to pay shop prices. These would make enough for a burger at least."

"I wanted them for my wife. She's very ill in hospital."

"Oh, sorry. You have them, Mister."

"No, you!"

"Why don't we share them?" The girl began to divide the bunch in two.

"No, I've a better idea. Let's put the flowers back and you come home with me. I can give you a warmer coat—you're the same size as my wife, or maybe a bit smaller. And how about a cup of tea and a cheese-and-pickle sandwich?"

Sitting at his kitchen table, the girl, Liz, told him more about herself. She'd run away from home. She was fifteen.

"Why, just the right age to be my granddaughter."

"Have you got grandkids?"

"No. Beryl and I weren't blessed with children. But we've had a happy life apart from that."

"So had I till Dad died and Mum took up with Clint. Clint keeps trying to interfere with me when he's been drinking."

Together, they phoned social services, who said they'd find somewhere for Liz to stay. Arthur sensed that they didn't trust him with her. Such times we live in, he thought, when an old chap of eighty-five is automatically suspect.

Just before she left with the social worker, Liz remembered something important. She spoke to Arthur out of the car window.

"My dad died in hospital. There weren't any flowers on the ward and I asked why not, and the nurse said they don't allow them nowadays."

"Thank you for telling me that, Liz."

As they waved goodbye, Arthur thought how small and fragile she looked in Beryl's best navy-blue coat with the furry collar turned up.

Next day, Arthur took Beryl a large Valentine's card. He told her about Liz, saying he'd found the girl huddled on the doorstep, and made Beryl smile as he described her wolfing down the cheese sandwich and almost disappearing in the navy-blue coat.

"You make me proud, my dear," Beryl whispered. "You're a good man, Arthur."

The end

**The Grave Robbers** was first published in *Scribble Magazine*, Summer 2013. It won 3rd prize in *Scribble* Readers' Choice Competition and was inspired by a news report of someone prosecuted for stealing flowers from graves. It was also winner of the *First Writer Magazine* Short Story Competition, 2014. Reproduced in Issue 26 Winter 2014/15.

# Out of the Sea

Tamsin Treadwell walked up the high moorland, bright with gorse. She paused and turned now and then to look down over the small fields with their ancient granite walls, towards the little village of Zennor. This was the place she'd most wanted to see in all the world. She stopped to rest on the hilltop beside the huge Neolithic burial chamber known as the Zennor Quoit.

Tamsin was spending a legacy from her grandmother on a year of travel. She hoped to return to Los Angeles with material for her master's thesis, to be called *Mermaids: a myth and its origins*. It would take in history, literature and art, as well as marine biology, the subject she'd studied up till now. Everything pointed to Cornwall in the far west of England.

Tamsin's professor expected her to research the mating habits of the polygamous grey seal and the monogamous long-snouted seahorse, but Tamsin was more interested in the mermaid legends: ambiguous, thrilling and seemingly universal. She didn't tell the professor that because of her Cornish roots and her connection to a certain Matthew Trewella of Zennor, she longed to see the church where he sang so sweetly that a mermaid came out of the sea to listen, and fell in love with him.

Tamsin had been preoccupied with this story since her father told her about Matthew and his mermaid bride. He said that an ancestor, a tin miner by the name of Thomas Trewella, migrated to California in the nineteenth century, and changed his name to Treadwell. There was a Treadwell tradition that this Thomas came from the same family as Matthew Trewella, the most famous person ever lured away by a mermaid. Tamsin, then aged six, asked if she was a descendant of Matthew's.

"Of course not, Tamsin," said her father. "That would mean you'd be some sort of weird sea creature. But I suppose both you and I have a few of the same genes as Matthew."

"But I'm not part-mermaid?"

"Nope. Sorry, honey!"

\* \* \*

When Tamsin announced her travel plans, her parents raised objections.

"Wouldn't it be easier to go to Florida and look at the manatees? I thought *they* were the original mermaids," said her mother.

But they softened when Tamsin mentioned Matthew and Zennor.

So she flew to England. Driving through Cornwall, she got diverted by tales of the Beast of Bodmin Moor and by all the quoits and menhirs and barrows scattered around the moorland landscape. None of the locals she met could help with her research, and she learned nothing about mermaids that she couldn't have found on the Internet. But Cornwall had her under its spell.

She stopped briefly in Padstow, Seaton and Lamorna, places with mermaids of their own, but mermaids whose stories were about cruelty and revenge. Then she headed for Zennor, home of the loveliest legend of them all.

In Zennor she took a room at the inn, the thirteenth-century Tinners' Arms. There were old flagstones in the bar, and outside a footpath followed a little stream to Pendour Cove below. It was in this cove that the mermaid Moreven met a ship's captain and told him that she'd married Matthew Trewella in her own country beneath the sea. And it was here that Matthew and Moreven sang their warnings of stormy weather.

On her first day, Tamsin walked over to the church, St Senara's, little and grey, its no-nonsense square tower dominating the tiny village. Matthew's singing in this church enticed the mermaid Moreven out of the sea. He carried her back in his arms, and both of them vanished under the waves. Tamsin found the old carving of the mermaid holding a little round mirror and combing her hair.

The Vicar, a member of the Old Cornwall Society, was quick to tell her that stories of wreckers luring ships on to the rocks with false lights were unfair and untrue. But he conceded that Cornish people did say that prayer:

*Oh please Lord, let us pray for all at sea.*

*But if there's got to be wrecks, please send them to we.*

But Matthew Trewella and his mermaid bride did their best to prevent wrecks hereabouts. They sang soft and high when the weather was going to be fair, and loud and low when storms were due. The life of many a Zennor fisherman was preserved because of their singing.

"Matthew Trewella is quite recent history," said the Vicar, "And I fear his mermaid isn't history at all. Nice story, though! Now up there, you'll find the Zennor Quoit. That's real history."

\* \* \*

Exploring the burial chamber brought to mind the uncounted generations before Matthew Trewella and in all the years after him.

"Our time is so brief," thought Tamsin, "Am I using mine well?"

Her reflections were interrupted by the sight of a graceful white yacht, which cast anchor out at sea. It seemed to be some sort of omen. She made a decision.

She would base herself in Zennor; here, she'd observe the seals and plan her thesis. But maybe, during her time in Cornwall, she would come to choose a different path in life.

The Tinners' Arms landlord helped her to find a cottage to rent. She joined the small church choir; like Matthew, Tamsin had a fine singing voice.

Every morning Tamsin took the path to the Cove and sat among the sea pinks watching for seals. One day at high tide she spotted a pair of seals bottling. With their funny whiskers and dog-like faces, how could anyone mistake them for mermaids? She'd read somewhere that singing to seals would get a response, so she practised the hymn for next Sunday, one she knew well, back home called 'The Navy Hymn':

*Eternal Father, strong to save …*
*Oh hear us when we cry to thee*
*For those in peril on the sea.*

The seals paid no attention, but from below came a fine tenor voice joining in her song.

Then she saw a swimmer hauling himself out of the sea and up the rocks. He had golden hair. His muscles rippled and his tanned body glistened in the sunshine. Tamsin stopped singing.

He called up to her, "What a lovely voice you have! I couldn't keep away. May I come and talk to you?" She detected just a hint of an Australian accent.

"Of course you can," she said. He came and sat on the turf beside her.

"What are you doing? I saw you were taking notes," he said.

Tamsin pointed to the seals. "I'm trying to work out whether they're courting or just good friends." Then she asked, "What brings you here from Down Under?"

He told her he owned the white yacht she'd seen lying at anchor. He'd spent several months at sea.

"How do you make a living?" Tamsin enquired. And then she was sorry; it was the sort of question her tactless mother would have asked.

"I —er—I've been fortunate. I'm taking some time off to see the world and try to make plans for the rest of my life. I'd like to be a bit more useful but I don't yet know how. Maybe I should go back to university."

"What will you study?"

"I'm thinking about some professional training: medicine, perhaps. Or I might take courses that would help me administer the funds I've inherited—I want to make the best use of them I possibly can. Find the right charities, make the money work hard …" He paused, looking embarrassed, then said quickly, "But now it's your turn. Tell me more about yourself. It's not every day I come across a mysterious American beauty spying on seals off the Cornish coast."

"I've just graduated. Trying to do some research for my master's thesis. But I can't settle down to it. The sea and the Cornish light seem to mesmerise me. Instead of working I walk the coastal path and explore the prehistoric sites. And

I've joined the Zennor church choir ... Oh, by the way, my name's Tamsin."

"I'm Tristan."

Tamsin smiled at him. "We both have Cornish names."

"Yes. One of my ancestors was a tinner from Cornwall. We ended up owning some gold mines in Western Australia. Have you got Cornish roots, too?"

Tamsin told him about her ancestor Thomas Trewella and about Matthew Trewella and the mermaid.

"You know, Tamsin, I think you've inherited the Trewella singing gene. I'd love to come to the service and hear you."

That Sunday she sang her best, knowing that he was there, but tried to avoid looking at him. He was sitting at the back of the church, his eyes closed. When he opened them after the last words of *Eternal Father, Strong to Save*, she saw that they were fixed on her face.

After church they walked up to the Quoit.

"The service was beautiful," he said.

"Are you a believer?"

"Not in the usual sense," he said, "but in a place like this with a woman like you ... well, sometimes I believe in magic."

* * *

Not long after that, Tamsin Treadwell left the village, but she did not return to Los Angeles.

E-mails arrived. Tamsin's parents were astonished to learn that she was sailing the seven seas with an Australian multi-millionaire.

And the Cornish branch of the Royal National Lifeboat Association was overjoyed to receive a cheque for a million

Australian dollars. In their own way, Tamsin and her sweetheart from Down Under were following the example of Matthew Trewella and Moreven the mermaid: they were helping those in peril on the sea.

The end

**Out of the Sea** was first published by Ether Books Ltd, 2012. I grew up in Cornwall, and Zennor is one of my favourite places.

# The Auction

"It might not work, of course," said my best friend, Virginia.

We had both been accepted by our first-choice university and we were unhappy about being saddled with huge student loans.

"Auctioning our virginity on EBay might pay for our fees," she went on.

We did it.

Virginia's virginity was bought by a Mr Biggs. I caught a glimpse of him as he arrived at our flat to claim his purchase. He was an ugly, dissolute-looking fellow.

The man who bought mine was handsome and kind as well as extremely rich: Max LeFèvre, heir to a substantial fortune. "I don't want your virginity," he wrote, "but I want you to have the money." We met, we dated, and I fell madly in love.

Not long afterwards, things fell apart.

Virginia took ill and was diagnosed with a nasty sexually transmitted disease. My beloved Max left me, gently and kindly, the way he'd treated me all along. I became severely depressed.

Virginia and I both failed our first-year exams and had to leave university. Now we share a flat in Bolton and we're doing a catering course at the local college and bar work in the evenings.

We avoid men and stick together. At least we have each other. You may think we've learned a useful lesson. Perhaps we have, but I don't know what it is.

The end


**The Auction** was first published in *Records, Rivers and Rats: poetry and flash fiction,* Early Works Press, 2018. It was inspired by a news report about a girl auctioning her virginity on E-bay.

# Please Call Me Jessica

I'm dreading this, but it's got to be done, thought Jessica, as she opened the door. She tried not to wince as she walked forward in her tight shoes, the first high heels she had ever worn. The rest of her outfit was what's called 'gender-neutral': a grey trouser suit and a white shirt. She approached the oversized desk with the portly white-haired man looking across at her from his huge leather chair. Mr Hetherington motioned her to take a seat, nodded, and said, "Well now, what is it you wanted to see me about, James?"

"Please, Mr Hetherington, call me Jessica," she said, in her low, husky voice.

"Jessica. My apologies. I can't get used to it." She noticed a flush rising above his collar, slowly covering his jowls and cheeks. She wondered if it was displeasure or embarrassment. He blew his nose and wiped his glasses with his handkerchief.

They were silent for a moment. Then Jessica spoke in a rush, looking down at the floor.

"I have to ask for a month's unpaid leave," she said. "After Christmas. If you wish, I'll find a temporary replacement and show them the ropes."

Another silence. Mr Hetherington cleared his throat.

"But Jame–Jessica. Are you not aware that the New Year is our busiest time? I call it the dying season. All those old people passing away. Wills to be read. Estates to be administered. And, as far as I recall, you've been with us less than a year."

"If you say no, I'd quite understand, but I'm afraid I'd have to resign."

"That would be highly regrettable. You are a valued member of the firm. I don't wish to be intrusive, but I have to enquire why you are making this request … because if you are planning a world cruise … or is it something to do with your family?"

"It's for my operation, Mr Hetherington."

"Oh, my dear boy. I'm so sorry. I had no idea …"

"Oh, I'm not ill. It's just that, well, you probably didn't realise, but I've been on a course of hormone therapy … and now I've come to the final stage, and, well … it's called gender reassignment surgery."

"Please. You don't need to go into the details. In fact, I'd rather you didn't."

"So it's all right, then? I have your permission?"

"Oh, yes, yes."

"And my therapist has advised me to tell everyone in advance: when I come back to work, I'll be wearing women's clothes and I'll have changed my name legally."

"Very well. Very well. Let's say no more about it. Now, if you'll forgive me, I've a great deal to do this morning … " Mr Hetherington rose, moved round his desk, and opened the door for her. Jessica was glad to escape.

In the run-up to Christmas, no one asked Jessica to a party. She received a few Christmas cards, but did not reciprocate. And as they left the office early on Christmas Eve, no one seemed to know what to say to her. Most people settled for, "See you next year."

Christmas with her parents was difficult. They had more or less accepted her changing appearance and her new name, but they found it hard to call her their daughter.

At a party in the village, someone said, "Ah, Jessica, haven't you got a brother called James? I hear he's an up-and-coming solicitor with Hetherington and Son in Collingbridge." And Jessica replied, "That's me. But I'm Jessica now, not James." Her mother heard this exchange and turned away, visibly distressed.

Jessica tried to comfort her. "Oh Mum, don't take it so much to heart. No harm's done."

"I know, I know. I just can't bear to think of them sniggering about you."

"Let them. Your friends have got used to it already. And the others will soon find something else to snigger about."

Her mother nodded; but after that, her parents cried off further drinks parties and stopped inviting people to their house.

On Christmas Day, Jessica came down to breakfast wearing a skirt. Her father and mother both looked embarrassed but they made no mention of it. Her mother's presents to her included some lipstick and perfume, and she almost wept with gratitude. She was coming to realise something she had only known intellectually: that having their son become their daughter required her parents to draw on huge reserves of courage and love.

When January came and she returned to her flat in Collingbridge, Jessica was beginning to wonder: this new life of hers, wouldn't it be easier in another town, in a new job?

"Think it over carefully," said her therapist. "Would moving on again be the answer? You have done so well. The voice training, learning to walk like a woman, and now the clothes. I'd like you to think about what else you need to make a go of it."

Jessica knew: she needed friendship and support. Soon after starting work at Hetherington and Son, she had informed her new colleagues that she was becoming a woman; but after that, her conversation had been confined to work. She hadn't noticed whether they wanted to be friendly or not. In fact, a few of them had asked her to join them at the pub after work and she had refused. She'd stayed away from the farewell drinks for Jenny – or was it Janet? – their much-loved coffee lady, and hadn't even contributed to the leaving present. Her preoccupation with the sex change had made her self-absorbed and thoughtless. She felt ashamed when she realised that she couldn't remember what sort of cancer Dave had got, or which of Annie's parents had died. No wonder she felt isolated—she had isolated herself.

After the operation, Jessica spent a few days alone in her flat, mulling over the challenges she now faced. She telephoned her therapist and talked through the course of action she had devised. Then she emailed her colleagues one by one.

'Just a note to say I'm looking forward to coming back to work in March. Now that James has really gone and I am really Jessica, I want to apologise to you for the way I have been focussing on this to the exclusion of almost everything else. I would like to try and make amends for my unsociable behaviour. Could you come round to my place for an informal supper?'

In each message she inserted an extra sentence: 'sorry I didn't make it to your Halloween party', 'thank you for your

Christmas card', 'hoping your son got that place at University'—the things she had neglected to say to them before.

Everyone accepted her invitation: the other solicitors, the administrative staff, the clerks. She dared not invite Mr Hetherington. He was so old-fashioned, so set in his ways, he had probably never heard of transsexuals till he found himself employing one, and, anyway, he had often said he did not think it proper to socialise with his staff.

After much hesitation, Jessica decided to wear her skirt; but when the time came she switched back to the trouser suit. She ordered in some enormous pizzas and followed them with ice cream and chocolate sauce. They talked about music, books, holidays and families. She didn't say out loud, "I'm not just a transsexual solicitor; there's more to me than that. And I want to make friends." Nonetheless, she felt that her message was getting across.

For her return to work, Jessica wore a green dress that set off her auburn shoulder-length hair. A stranger would not have guessed she had been a man, except for her Adam's apple, and that was concealed with a cream silk scarf. True, she had large hands and feet, but so had lots of women, she told herself, and small breasts and slim hips were fashionable nowadays. She feared stares from her fellow passengers on the bus but saw none, and the new receptionist at the front desk said "Good Morning" in a perfectly normal manner.

Jessica shut herself in her office, with an 'engaged' notice on the door; she was still nervous of appearing in women's clothes in front of her colleagues. She spent the day sorting her mail and reading the new cases she'd been allocated. Lunch was a sandwich at her desk.

At four o'clock the phone rang. A summons from Mr Hetherington: "Jessica, would you come to my office, please?" Polite and formal, as always.

I'm dreading this, she thought once again, recalling that awkward interview before her operation.

But as she opened the door, she heard chatter and music and found the room full of people. Mr Hetherington was standing in front of his desk. He handed her a glass of champagne.

"Here's to new beginnings, Jessica, my dear," said Mr Hetherington. "We all wish you happiness in your new life."

It was unlikely that he'd undergone a sudden change of heart and planned this little party on his own initiative, Jessica thought. No doubt someone had been educating him. But she didn't mind. She smiled at him and sipped her champagne. "Thank you, Mr Hetherington."

Mr Hetherington swallowed his drink in one gulp, and addressed the whole company, his face pink, his brow dripping with perspiration. "Please, everyone, let's try to be a little less formal. Hetherington and Son must move with the times. I'd like you to drop the 'Mr Hetherington'. From now on I want you all to call me James."

The end

**Please Call Me Jessica** was runner-up in the Wells Short Story Competition, 2018. I wrote it after I had attended a party for a transgender friend to celebrate the start of her new life.

# Do you Remember the Barn Owl?

A scream. A silence. And then a squeal. As she waits in the lane, the child shudders though she knows these are just the familiar night sounds of fields and woods around her home. Patience, she tells herself. Be patient, soon the bird will come. With not the faintest whisper of wings, it will fly along the fence beside the field. The barn owl, the silent hunter. The owl is white below, but its feathers are buff-brown above. Yet it looks pure white, ghostly white. The heart-shaped face is beautiful and cruel.

The roost is in a ruined farmhouse beyond the wheat field. Built and abandoned in the seventeenth century, this was home to a couple with children but no further descendants. The house stands among trees, and when the wind stirs the branches and the moon shines overhead, you can sometimes see shadows move inside and imagine pale faces at the empty windows. A local historian says the family was probably wiped out by the Great Plague, though how the Plague reached this isolated spot is hard to guess. Others in the village claim the house was the scene of multiple murder and suicide. But there are no records to confirm either account.

"They probably just moved away," said the girl's father when she asked about these stories.

"Anyway, we don't believe in ghosts," her mother added quickly, which made her uneasy; she had not thought of ghosts till then. Since that conversation she has kept away from the old farmhouse, and after sunset she tries not to look in that direction.

She is nervous in the dark. On winter evenings she hurries home from the bus stop, trying to ignore the country noises that make her tremble although she knows them well. Beneath the hedgerow small rodents rustle among the weeds, and birds tweet sleepily in the bushes. Pigeons startled by her footsteps rise up with a great clatter of wings. From the woods come the hoot of tawny owls, the bark of foxes and deer, and sometimes the piteous squeal of a doomed rabbit. Once she heard badgers fighting, a sickening cacophony of yelps and growls. Even when she's safe and cosy in her bed, with a little cat-shaped nightlight glowing on the dresser and her parents in the room below, these sounds make her shiver.

Yet on some nights the lonely little girl conquers her fear and comes out to see the barn owl. There might be a pair; she can't be sure, though she never sees two at once. If there's a pair, it is usually the male who hunts while the female remains at the roost. Afraid of the dark and the ruined farmhouse, but she doesn't fear the barn owl—her father says the only creature that need be afraid of owls is the little vole bustling about in the undergrowth. The child is sorry for the vole and half-hopes it will survive another night. But she understands that owls must eat.

On this night, while she is waiting, the child hears voices and laughter in the lane—two boys from the village. She recognises the voices—nice boys, who are in the class above hers and travel to school on the same bus. Are they, like her, interested in owls? Is that why they are here?

She wishes she could join them and share the excitement of watching the owl. If they become friends, she could show them the badger sett, the tree where the tawny owl sleeps by day, the spot by the stream where her father once saw an otter. In daylight they could venture into the old farmhouse and look for the barn owl roost—if the boys were with her she wouldn't worry about the ghosts.

But she has never dared speak to the boys and she is too shy to approach them now; she crouches behind a large hawthorn at the side of the lane.

When the boys come into view, she sees there's a man with them. He is carrying a crossbow and arrows. "Is this the place?" he asks quietly and when the boys say yes he tells them roughly to shut up.

The man and the boys take up position beside the fence. The child realises what they are planning; she's seen a stuffed barn owl in a shop window. She is afraid, for the owl and for herself, and panicky and confused. As the muddle in her head clears, one thing becomes obvious: she should try to stop this. If she scares the owl off it surely will not return this night. From beyond the field she hears the owl's eerie screech as it leaves its home in the farmhouse.

To alert the owl and save its life she has only to stand up and wave her arms and call hello to the boys. Yet she does nothing. She remains frozen, crouched motionless in the shadows. She seems to be paralysed—her voice won't shout and her limbs won't move.

The owl flies towards them and the man pulls an arrow from his canvas knapsack, raises his bow, places the arrow, and takes aim. The girl opens her mouth to cry out, but no sound comes. The man shoots. The pale body falls and the man jumps over the fence; he yanks out the arrow and blood spurts from the wound and stains the lovely white breast feathers. Laughing, the man picks up the corpse. "Show's over!" The two boys are silent for a moment and then they too begin to laugh. The man claps them on the back and they do the same to him, like grown-up mates. Then they high-five each other, the boys getting blood on their palms. The man stuffs the dead owl in his knapsack. Still laughing, they turn and disappear down the lane.

It is spring, so there may well be young birds at the roost. If there were two owls, the dead owl's mate will take over as provider. The next night the girl watches for hours, hoping to see a second, widowed owl. In vain—it seems there was only one.

The evening after that, the little girl borrows her father's torch. Telling herself to be brave, she crosses the field to the farmhouse ruins. She feels driven to find out if there are owlets awaiting their parent's return. Beyond this, she has no clear purpose, but it somehow seems the right thing to do.

There's a wooden gate where the front door used to be. The ground floor houses abandoned farming stuff: a rusted ploughshare, a tractor box, a single broken wheel. The dusty air makes her cough and the sound disturbs some unseen creatures—there's scuttling and a couple of squeaks. Two small dark things whisk from behind one straw bale and vanish into another. A stack of straw half-conceals a huge fireplace with an ancient bread oven. She steps into the fireplace and peers up the chimney, shining the torch. Her hand is shaking and the beam wobbles as it illuminates the chimney—nothing but bare blackened walls. She treads on something soft and lets out a cry, but it's only a piece of sacking, the size of a human being.

The owl, she remembers, would exit from an upper window.

Compelled to go up, she looks around for the staircase. There is none, only a wooden ladder with an open hatch at the top. She climbs the ladder slowly, with a stupid feeling that at any moment an arm—or an angry bird—might emerge from the hatch and knock her down, or some sharp-toothed creeping thing might attack from below. She hauls herself through the hatch on to a strong wooden floor. This space too has been used for storage: a coil of rope, rusty tools, and a rotting cardboard box with a doll's head peeping over the top, a china head with big round eyes. She takes a closer look; the doll's cloth body is in shreds, and a toy bear beside it has ears and limbs but nothing else except its dusty glass eyes.

Another fireplace. And high up, on a shelf, she can make out two small whitish shapes, rocking slowly back and forth: owlets. She hears the owlets' strange snoring calls. They are begging for food, but she has nothing to give them.

The light is fading now. As if pursued, she half-climbs, half-tumbles down the ladder and runs across the field and down the lane to her home.

The only answer is to tell the grown-ups. Bird lovers themselves, her parents would surely arrange a rescue, take the owlets to the owl sanctuary. But how could she bring herself to confess that she had watched the killing of the adult bird and done nothing when she could have saved it? No, she will not tell anyone, ever. Fear of disgrace overrides her compassion for those baby owls.

A week later she returns to the farmhouse, dreading what she will find, yet needing to know the outcome. In that upper room there is only silence and the small white shapes are lying still. The horror of it, she thinks, is the punishment she has deserved.

\* \* \*

Ten years have passed. The young woman has come to stay with her parents. She's a student now. She has never lost her love of wildlife.

She's just back from a trip to Malta with fellow birders. It was the end of April, in the two weeks of Malta's spring hunt, the time when migrating birds pass over the island on their way to breed. The birders sighted a flock of dainty soft-coloured turtle doves and were delighted; an endangered species none of them had seen before.

A truck approached and pulled up right next to them. Half a dozen hunters with dogs and guns emerged. The young woman and her friends shouted and gesticulated but they were manhandled and pushed roughly aside. One of the hunters made a phone call and minutes later the police arrived from the nearby village. Each group accused the other of assault, and the Maltese authorities finally allowed both the hunters and the bird-watchers to leave.

The young woman has come home bruised, but defiant and angry. Her parents have read about the episode in the newspaper. They think one ought to respect the cultural traditions of other countries. "You and your friends should mind your own business."

And she replies, "No. Protecting wildlife matters more than your dislike of judging other people's cultures. And there's the cruelty — a lot of birds aren't killed outright and they die a horrible slow death. We felt we must stand and be counted. We should do what we know is right even when we're afraid. That's what you taught me."

"We know how much you care about birds. Do you

remember the barn owl? For years you went out regularly to see it. Then you suddenly stopped; you seemed to lose interest. It's sad—nobody has seen a barn owl round here since then."

She walks to the derelict farmhouse. Like a killer needing to visit my victim's grave, she thinks; yet she has not felt this compulsion until now, ten years after the event. The confrontation in Malta has reminded her of that time she failed to stand up for what she knew to be right.

The old house has fallen further into ruin. The gate has gone from the doorway. Ivy and elder have invaded, and the dank air reeks of rotting vegetation. But the ladder is still sturdy and she climbs up. A pair of jackdaws fly out of an upstairs window and she is suddenly afraid.

In the empty upper room she fancies she hears a snapping beak and an angry hiss.

Not yet forgiven.

## The end

**Do You Remember the Barn Owl?** This was a guest post on the Mark Avery Blog *"Standing up for Wildlife"* 2022. I grew up on a farm where there was a ruined farmhouse with resident barn owls. The story was inspired by the news of broadcaster Chris Packham protesting against the massacre of birds in Malta.

# Brief Encounter 2011

A railway station isn't like an airport. A few meeters and greeters, but not so much exuberance, fewer demonstrations of love. More bad tempers on show. Late trains and inaudible announcements.

There's a stench from the men's loos. The Ladies' seems to have been visited by a pack of those puppies who like nothing better than a long, strong roll of toilet paper.

But the station is warm. You can read. And write. She's drafting a letter to another would-be soulmate from *playingaway.com*, the dating agency that matches people who want to cheat on their partner.

How many has she met here? How many times has she felt tempted to do a runner?

She's heard of it happening, usually when people had agreed to meet in a pub or café. Mostly it was the man who took a quick look and scarpered when he saw his disappointing date clutching the pre-arranged newspaper. Not that this could happen to her. Smiling to herself, she stretches out her long shapely legs and runs scarlet-tipped fingers through her glossy black locks.

She hasn't always been a stunner. In fact, before her diet and her makeover, she had one embarrassing experience at a station. They failed to recognise each other from the photos on the dating site and stood side by side, each holding a *Times* and talking crossly on their mobile phones:

"Look, I'm outside Burger King as we agreed."

"No, *I'm* outside Burger King. You must be somewhere else."

Eventually they turned to each other and made polite excuses and tried to make it into a joke. Unable to tell the truth: that they both looked older, fatter and plainer than expected.

This time will be different. He's sure to look her up and down, they can't stop themselves. A bit uncomfortable, but she'll do the same to him. Fair's fair.

He'll fancy her, she doesn't doubt it. And if she fancies him, she'll ask him back to her flat. The camera is set up in readiness. And she's bought a fresh supply of Viagra, just in case. She looks forward to her fat fee from the porno magazine. He won't dare demand a cut—far from it: she hopes to extract a fee from him as well, a reward for not blabbing to his wife.

The train arrives on time. She stands up on her killer heels and gets ready to smile.

The end

**Brief Encounter, 2011** was first published in *Click to Click: Tales of Internet Dating*, ed. Barbara Lorna Hudson 2012. It was written at Oxford station, waiting to meet an Internet date, but is entirely fictional.

# Patricia and the Slasher

"Why don't we try Internet dating?" said Rosy.

"Because you never know who you might meet ... a cheating husband, a fraudster, maybe even a serial killer," said Ann.

"You could meet any of those at a drinks party," Patricia countered.

"And how many drinks parties do *we* get invited to? I haven't had an invitation for years. Nobody wants extra women over sixty," said Rosy. She paused and then added thoughtfully, "But I suppose being introduced by a computer is quite a scary idea."

The three friends were sitting at Patricia's kitchen table, sipping their wine and wishing they had some male company. They clustered round the computer and Rosy showed the others how to search for a date online.

"They're all evil-looking or decrepit," said Ann. "And most of them want women ten years younger than themselves. What a nerve they've got!"

"Well, we may not be sex goddesses exactly, but we're not that bad for our age," said Rosy. "Let's check out the competition."

They did another search, signing in as men seeking women. The results came as a shock: there were hordes of beautiful, bubbly, fun-loving sixtyish women and they far outnumbered the sixtyish men.

By the end of the evening, Rosy and Ann had chickened out. "Let's go on a singles holiday instead," said Rosy.

Patricia, however, summoned up her courage, wrote an enticing profile and uploaded some flattering photos. She was sure she could spot the fraudsters, the cheats and the psychopaths. And she resolved not to take anything her dates said at face value. As a further safeguard, she promised to keep Rosy and Ann informed of whom she was meeting, and where and when.

"That probably won't save me," she said, "but I suppose it might help with police enquiries after I disappear." Rosy laughed but Ann didn't.

The first person to contact Patricia was a retired solicitor called Carlo who had a golden retriever called Mandy. ("A man who *says* he is a retired solicitor and *says* he has a golden retriever called Mandy," Patricia told herself sternly.) They talked at length on the phone. Each ticked all the other's boxes: agnostic, bookish, on the wrong side of sixty and the wrong side of average weight. Neither claimed to be very rich or very poor. Both were widowed. Best of all: Carlo could make her laugh.

He suggested coming to Oxford for lunch and an afternoon walk. And she suggested that he bring Mandy, "I'm sure she'll help break the ice."

"What ice?" said Carlo.

At the station Mandy immediately proved the point by making friendly overtures to any passer-by who so much as glanced at her. Patricia was charmed. And Carlo seemed nice as well.

"You're every bit as pretty as your photo," he said, beaming at her and shaking her hand vigorously. He was short and wide, but she liked his curly grey hair and his big smile, and answered, "You're not so bad yourself."

They walked along the river to *The Butcher's Arms*. In the

pub, beside the fire, Patricia caught Carlo studying her when he should have been studying the menu; and later, when she pointed out some great crested grebes, she noticed that Carlo was watching her with more interest than he gave to the grebes. As they watched Mandy scattering the gulls and ducks and plovers on the flooded meadow, he took her hand; and the setting sun painted sky and water golden red.

Patricia broke the safety rules her friends had laid down and invited Carlo to her house for high tea (a perfect Spanish omelette she'd made earlier, just in case). Then she saw them off at the station, giving Mandy a cuddle and Carlo a hug. Mandy barked and tried to disrupt the hug.

"She's jealous," said Carlo. "She doesn't like the idea of somebody else being my Number One Girl."

Next day was Sunday and the three friends met for coffee as usual. Rosy and Ann wanted to hear every detail about the date with Carlo.

True to form, Ann was suspicious. "What sort of a name is 'Carlo'? Sounds like something a crook would call himself. Have you checked his credentials as a solicitor?"

But Rosy saw possibilities: "A man with a nice dog can't be all bad. He didn't leap on you over tea, and he must like you or he'd have gone home earlier."

They talked about Christmas. Rosy was off to Cornwall and Ann to Norfolk, to their grown-up children. Patricia planned to celebrate alone with her collection of old Hitchcock films.

"Invite Carlo," said Rosy.

"You surely wouldn't be so rash!" said Ann.

"If only I knew him better," said Patricia. "If things work out for us we'll be spending every Christmas together in future. But it's early days—I hardly know the man."

"Well, you'd better get a move on —this is a perfect opportunity," said Rosy.

"A perfect opportunity for *what?*" said Ann darkly.

Patricia found it difficult. "What are you doing for Christmas, Carlo?"

"Oh, I'll probably eat too much, drink whisky and watch DVDs."

"On your own?"

"Afraid so."

"You may think this is a crazy idea: but what about coming here? And bring Mandy, of course. You could stay in my spare room." She was glad he couldn't see her red face.

He didn't seem surprised and accepted right away.

On Christmas Eve Patricia met them off the train. Carlo had a huge backpack, Mandy on her lead, a plastic bag overflowing with sweaters and books and dog food, and a large wicker carrying basket. From the basket came an angry, piercing miaow. Through the gaps in the weave Patricia could make out bright little eyes and a funny little face with a black nose poking out.

Carlo looked embarrassed. "The cattery was fully booked, so I thought … I tried to ring you before I left home but you weren't answering … I couldn't leave him."

There was just time to rush to the supermarket for cat food and cat litter. They found an old tin tray in the shed and turned it into a cat's toilet.

His name was Jack and he was a fluffy black and white bundle of nerves. He tore round the house in terror of Patricia, and for recreation scratched furiously at every chair and sofa he could find. Patricia covered them with sheets one by one till her lounge looked like a stately home in the closed season. But still you could hear frenzied ripping sounds as a small bulge moved between sheet and furniture.

Carlo and Patricia's Christmas hug was interrupted by a disgruntled Mandy. They settled down to watch *Psycho* and as they brought their armchairs closer, Jack appeared to have a change of heart. He climbed on to Patricia's lap. Patricia felt honoured. She began stroking and he purred sweetly. She leaned towards Carlo, "Look. I think Jack likes me." As she spoke, the cat twisted round with a hiss, and slash!—he produced a long, deep scratch mark and a trickle of blood, and then rushed away.

While Patricia washed the wound and applied antiseptic cream, Carlo apologised. "He's so unpredictable! I ought to have warned you. He's done it to me, too, but I always forgive him. It's a sort of reflex: he just panics. He can't help it."

I like a man who can forgive, thought Patricia. But I'd prefer a cat who can control himself. Why aren't there any cat-training manuals?

On New Year's Eve, Patricia dragged herself to the surgery, feeling rotten, afraid she'd caught cat scratch fever. The doctor reassured her. "No swollen glands. Don't worry, it's only flu."

Carlo got flu as well. When they'd recovered they met again, at Carlo's house in Birmingham. Mandy welcomed Patricia enthusiastically, spinning round with her tail wagging so hard it almost toppled her over. As soon as Patricia sat down, Jack jumped on her lap and started to purr. This time Patricia was cautious. No sudden moves; she made sure he knew she was about to stroke him; and she did it very gently. "My friends were afraid I'd meet a psychopath," she said. "And maybe I have. Jack's very cute for a slasher, though."

The end

**Patricia and the Slasher** was Highly Commended in Ifanca Helene James Short Story Competition, 2012 and was first published by Ether Books Ltd, 2012. Based on an Internet dating experience, much of this story was later incorporated in my novel *Timed Out* (2016). "Mandy" is a portrait of a real dog, except that she was a Labrador, not a Golden Retriever.

# Merry-go-round

Laura scurried along, thrusting through the crowds, in too much of a rush to marvel at the Biggest Dipper in the Known Universe. At the end of St Giles, she stopped and looked wildly around.

To her dismay, her colleague Alexandra lumbered towards her. "Fancy seeing you here!" Laura gave a half-smile and continued peering this way and that.

"What's the matter, Laura?"

"I'm looking for the carousel."

"They've put it somewhere else. Near the Museum, back the way you came. Why so concerned?"

"I'm not."

"And why so secretive?"

"I'm not, but I'm in a hurry."

Alexandra caught sight of another colleague and turned away. Relieved, Laura made her escape.

The music of the steam organ led her to the painted wooden horses, rising and falling on their gilded poles. Her eyes filled with tears. The carousel always affected her this way—some old memory, perhaps? She couldn't work it out. A recollection of the happiest days in her happy childhood?

Nearby was one of those roundabouts for younger children, miniature cars and a fire engine and a motorbike in bright primary colours, their little drivers pink with excitement, and proud parents watching. Laura noticed a toddler with blue dungarees and a mop of ginger curls. When the roundabout stopped, he was on the opposite side from his mother. He hopped down and scuttled off in the wrong direction. Laura rushed after the child as he moved towards the shooting booth across the way. She grabbed him and he yelled, "Mummy!"

Laura said, "Yes, we'll find your Mummy," and led him back.

"Thank you, thank you," his mother gushed, and launched into a list of excuses for her negligence. Laura managed to interrupt the woman and explain that she had an appointment. She glanced at her watch: 1.15 p.m. She fumbled for her purse and went to the man selling the carousel tickets. The appointed time. She was first to arrive.

Laura mounted a horse. She was the only customer.

A man approached the carousel and stopped. Each time Laura came level with him, she gazed at the handsome figure clutching a stick of candyfloss. To him, no doubt, she was near invisible, just a shapeless, grey-haired woman. She continued to ride around, paying again each time the ride ended. At 1.35 p.m., she saw the man give a slight shrug.

When the horses paused, he approached Laura and said, "Excuse me, have you seen this woman?" and pointed to a photograph on his iPhone.

His voice sounded just as warm and gentle as it had been on the telephone. Laura peered at the photo of her twenty-five-year-old self. She shook her head, and he walked away. A moment later he was back: "Do you happen to like candyfloss? I bought this for the woman I was meeting." Yes, she liked candyfloss.

Every August she joined the dating site *nolongerlonely.com*, lied about her age and uploaded the old photograph. And arranged a rendezvous beside the fairground carousel. Her birthday treat.

The end

**Merry-go-round** was first published in *Click to Click: Tales of Internet Dating*, ed. Barbara Lorna Hudson 2012. A nice lady I know does enjoy a ride by herself on the carousel, but she wouldn't dream of doing internet dating.

# The People Watcher and the Pile of Money

I was walking along St Giles. The man in front came to a sudden halt beside a bench by the Museum wall. He froze and stared at something under the bench: a heap of money, an untidy little pile, comprising a handful of pound coins and a few fifty-pence pieces, the silver gleaming in the sunlight caught through the slats.

I'm something of a mind-reader; I pride myself on it. I should have been a psychologist—or else a social worker, because I'm also a very caring person. I'm always looking for ways to benefit the community. I wish I could contribute more to the fight against crime. But there's not much an elderly lady can do in these violent times. However, I try my utmost to discourage the thoughtless behaviour I observe around me everywhere, every day.

Whenever I venture into town, I put on my "people-watcher" hat, so to speak. I had this young man down as a student. I moved a little, so that he noticed my presence; he straightened up and I caught his eye. He gave a shrug and walked quickly away.

"Good," I thought. "I've saved him from doing something wrong and I've protected someone's money."

I positioned myself beside the bench, not so close as to hide the coins, but close enough to make potential thieves uncomfortable. I feared there'd be many of these, and as usual I was right.

Next came a middle-aged couple.

"Look at that! Five pounds—"

"At least. Finders keepers—"

"Losers weepers." Then they noticed me watching them. As well as finishing each other's sentences they were obviously the sort of couple who can read each other's thoughts, for they departed without another word.

There followed a pair of teenaged girls wearing indecent skirts; when they bent over I could see their knickers. Then an older lady like myself, in a smart navy suit— disappointing to observe that she too was tempted. An overweight woman in garish clothes so tight she had difficulty bending down; a man in a wheelchair who couldn't get close enough to pick up the money anyway. There are lots of greedy people in Oxford. Respectably dressed or not, if someone saw the money there was the approach, the hesitation, the turning away when they realised they were being watched.

Quite a few people passed by without seeing the pile of money. Some were gawping at the buildings. Others were fully occupied gobbling their burgers and swilling over-priced American coffee or those drinks that stain your teeth.

One man threw down a sandwich wrapper and I handed it back to him with a polite "excuse me, you dropped this." He was wearing a tee shirt with 'I love Oxford' on it. He had the gall to say thank you. A woman yanked her poodle away from the bench with its leg still cocked when I cleared my throat loudly. A group of foul-mouthed youths and a quarrelling couple lowered their voices when I stared at them. I was having a civilising effect on this corner of Oxford.

It started to rain. I continued to stand here, trying to look as if I was waiting for someone.

People were hurrying to escape the rain and no one else

99

glanced in the direction of the money. I wondered what sort of person was irresponsible enough to go off and leave so much cash unattended. Drunk? On drugs? And how did he come by the cash? Begging, no doubt. Now, I'm one of those strong-minded individuals who never give to beggars as a matter of principle. In this country we give away more than enough via our taxes. Handing out money just encourages the beggars and they spend it on drugs and alcohol. They disfigure our beautiful city and make a bad impression on the tourists.

At long last someone approached who obviously knew the money was there. The beggar in question, no doubt. He was limping, with a bandage wrapped round his head, and his clothes were ragged and dirty. Obviously a non-worker. He must have fallen and banged his head while he was drunk. There was a foreign look about him, sort of swarthy or was it just dirt?

I didn't wait to find out. I scooped up the money and hurried away. This might stop him going on another drinking spree. I was doing him a favour. I didn't look back. He couldn't run after me, not with that limp, but I was surprised he didn't shout. He probably hasn't bothered to learn English.

I bought an evening paper.

*Asylum seeker victim of hit and run*

*An elderly man was injured by a hit and run driver at 3 am this morning. He had been sleeping on a bench near the Museum and was crossing the road to go the public conveniences. The victim is believed to be an asylum seeker who limps badly following his experiences in prison in his native country.*

So-called asylum seekers. That's another group the Government ought to deal with. They make up stories so as to get the benefits we British have worked all our lives for: social security, council houses, our wonderful national health service.

The driver should have stopped, of course. But the man shouldn't have been there. You don't expect pedestrians on the street at that time of night.

I considered giving the money to some charity, but I've heard how charities defraud the generous public. Charity begins at home, and I'm a pensioner.

The end

**The People Watcher and the Pile of Money** was first published in *Oxtale Soup: Stories of Oxford and Oxfordshire,* ed Sara Banerji, 2011. I once caught sight of a pile of cash under a bench in Oxford, but I just walked past.

# Barn, 1917

I push open the great doors slowly, reluctantly. They groan as if echoing my pain. The structure is still sound; if I could bring myself to have it converted we'd make a killing.

But this was his special place. He hid here when he'd been naughty. In the loft, behind the straw bales, or beneath the old cart. Just a child, and little more than a child when he went away.

Not much straw left. Who's going to bring in the bales from the next harvest and from all the harvests to come, after I am gone?

I hear a rustle and squeaking. Rats. They say there were rats *there* too—fatter and bolder than these ones.

The beams are sturdy and there's a coil of rope in the corner.

The end

**Barn, 1917.** This was homework set by creative writing teacher Sara Banerji: Write a flash fiction story about a barn and a war without mentioning "barn" or "war".

# The Last Night of the Proms

"It'll be like taking candy off a baby," said Cliff the lorry driver to his mate Derek. "Auntie Joan is daft as a brush and soft as butter. She'll be over the moon to see me. She'll hand over the dosh if I ask nicely."

Derek was unimpressed. "It's out of order to pretend to be a loving nephew and then take the poor old duck for a ride."

\* \* \*

"It'll be a doddle," said Mrs Joan Larkins' neighbour, Bob the burglar.

"That's as may be, but I don't like it," said his colleague Freddie, who didn't have much burgling experience and did have a soft spot for old ladies.

"Now listen up, you idiot," said Bob. "I'll go over it again. Upstairs in my place we climb the ladder into the roof space. We crawl along from house to house till we're above No.13, Mrs Larkins' house. There'll be a ladder there, just like mine, and we drop down from the loft. Then we check for drugs in the bathroom and take a look round her bedroom for jewellery."

"She might hear us. At her age the shock could kill her."

"She won't hear a thing. She plays that music real loud every night and anyway, she's deaf as a post. We won't go downstairs, so you needn't worry about scaring her."

"I still don't like it," said Freddie, "Count me out."

* * *

Bob and ninety-eight year old Mrs Larkins (Cliff's Great-Aunt Joan) lived in the same late-Victorian terrace in Kentish Town. It was nightfall on a September evening. His accomplice having backed out, Bob was at home by himself at No.1, laying out his burgling outfit neatly on his bed: black jeans and sweater, a black balaclava, and a pair of comfortable, quiet old trainers.

* * *

Cliff, too, was on his own, hammering at the dingy front door of Mrs Larkins' house, No.13.

"Hullo, Auntie Joan."

Mrs Larkins peered at Cliff—it was obvious she didn't recognize him.

"Remember your great-nephew Clifford? From Newcastle? I'm a long-distance lorry driver now. I'm in London overnight, thought I'd pay you a visit."

"Little Clifford! Lovely of you to come, pet. How you've grown! Let me get you a cup of tea. I've got some rock cakes left."

Mrs Larkins bustled around, chattering about her memories of the North East and about Cliff and his brother as children. He couldn't get a word in edgeways. Then she suddenly stopped and looked at the clock.

"Can you stay a while and listen to *The Last Night of the Proms* with me? The telly's broken down but the wireless is better for music anyway."

\* \* \*

An hour after the concert began, Bob was creeping along above the row of houses from No.1 to No.13. It was mainly straightforward, just an empty, dusty, spider-infested corridor, but here and there unexpected rafters and boxes and crates hindered his progress. He was afraid one of his neighbours below would detect the sounds above them, but he needn't have worried because everyone was in their front room glued to the telly. When he got to No.13 he found the noise from Mrs Larkins' radio deafening, even in the roof space. He crouched there for a few minutes, waiting for his ears to adjust sufficiently to pick out any movements beneath him. Then he levered open the trapdoor and let down the ladder to the landing below.

\* \* \*

Meanwhile, Cliff was stuck on Mrs Larkins' sofa sipping over-sweet tea and chewing an extremely old rock cake. *The Last Night of the Proms* was a confounded nuisance. Cliff kept trying to start a conversation about how skint he was and could Auntie Joan see her way to helping him out? Just a loan, on a purely temporary basis, of course.

But each time he began to speak, she shushed him. "Just let me hear this bit."

At around ten, there was a power cut.

Auntie Joan had no batteries for her radio. So that was the end of the concert. In the sudden silence, Cliff thought he heard a noise upstairs; it sounded almost like a man's voice saying, 'Hell!' But he decided he'd imagined it. His great-aunt felt her way into the kitchen in the darkness and returned with a candle perched precariously on a saucer.

Cliff stretched out his legs. He felt stiff and bored after sitting through nearly two hours of highbrow music. As Mrs Larkins passed the sofa she tripped over his legs and fell to the floor, the candle flame setting fire to her woollen dress. At the same moment the lights came on again, and the radio blared out *Land of Hope and Glory*.

Cliff didn't want his great-aunt to die—at least, not till she'd parted with some money and preferably not till she'd altered her will in his favour (step two of his Auntie Joan strategy).

He leapt up and beat out the flames. The fire was easily extinguished.

But so was Auntie Joan.

"Poor old dear!" said Cliff. After checking that she was really dead, he wiped away a tear and picked up the phone to summon an ambulance. Then he changed his mind: he'd just take a quick shufti, see if he could find any cash. He found five pounds in her handbag, a two-pound coin down the back of the sofa, and a jam jar full of silver in the kitchen. Then he decided to go and look under Auntie Joan's mattress.

He went upstairs. On the way up, he was caught short— due, no doubt, to the shock of losing his auntie so suddenly. He rushed past the loft ladder, wondering vaguely why it was down. The bathroom door was open and the light was on.

Inside the bathroom stood Bob, riffling through the medicine cupboard. The two men stared at each other, gasped, and spoke simultaneously, "Who are you?"

Then Cliff darted out again, grabbing the key. He turned it in the lock outside, leaving Bob alternately cursing and pleading and banging on the bathroom door.

As a result of this second shock, Cliff forgot the call of nature and forgot to look under the mattress. He hurried out of the house. Halfway down Albert Street he began to feel a little guilty. He didn't like to think of his great-aunt's body lying undiscovered. It might be a while before the burglar broke out of the bathroom, and could a villain like that be relied on to do the right thing? He might just scarper. Cliff wondered what he could do without getting involved with the authorities.

Cliff searched for his lorry, which he'd had to park several streets away. Then he drove up the Great North Road, keeping carefully within the speed limit, till he reached a service station. There he phoned the police, telling them they ought to pay a visit to 13 Albert Street, Kentish Town, and rang off before they could trace his call.

* * *

The Police were mightily surprised to find no signs of a break-in, a dead old lady in a singed dress in the lounge, and an angry man in black locked in the bathroom. The man in black insisted it wasn't the late Mrs Larkins who'd locked him in, but another man, a stranger. The police climbed up the loft ladder but found nothing.

It looked as though cash could have been taken from her handbag, but the man in black had no money on him. And the old lady had apparently set fire to herself with a candle during the power cut. Foul play was not suspected.

Interviewed at the Station, Bob explained that he was only being neighbourly, visiting poor old Mrs Larkins out of the goodness of his heart. He said he'd opened the loft trapdoor and pulled down the ladder in order to put in a few things she wanted out of the way. Then he'd asked permission to use her toilet. Although his dark clothes and nervous demeanour aroused their suspicions, the police couldn't think of anything to charge him with. They were unable to trace the caller who'd alerted them. That caller, they concluded, must be the mystery man who'd locked Bob in the bathroom and stolen the money.

\* \* \*

Reunited with their mates, both Bob and Cliff confessed that this had been a night they'd prefer to forget. They'd each had a shock and neither of them had made the easy financial gains they'd hoped for; they regretted the passing of old Mrs Larkins, kindly great-aunt and respected neighbour.

A prominent politician picked up the story and used it to illustrate the incompetence of English Electric, Southern Police and North London Social Services, though, when challenged, she was unable to say what any of them could have done to prevent the tragedy. After all, Mrs Larkins was ninety-eight, and a post-mortem confirmed that the cause of death was cardiac arrest.

The end

**The Last Night of the Proms** was first published by Ether Books Ltd, 2012. The idea came after a friend told me he'd heard someone moving along the shared attic space above his flat.

# Cleaning the Windows

'Bye bye, kitten. Kissy kissy.' He aims for her lips and, grimacing, she dodges her head sideways and makes him miss.

'Might be home a bit late.'

'Doesn't matter.'

Turning away, she grabs the bucket and swings it angrily, so that the soapy water spills over his neat flower bed.

She covers the windows in suds. Then she draws a curvy female shape on the glass and her frown disappears.

Water drips off the cloth into the cleavage of her full bosom. She glances down at herself and smiles and gently moves her free hand over her body.

The soap has loosened her wedding ring. She puts it in her pocket.

'I'm falling in love again,' she sings as she rubs the windows dry and polishes them to within an inch of their life.

The end

**Cleaning the Windows** was shortlisted in *Yellow Room Magazine* Competition, 2017. I must have been feeling anti-men at the time.

# How many Stars?

A two-star review on Amazon. "Not my sort of thing", it says, and pronounces my novel "too emotional and completely without interest". It's from a man, of course—not interested in love or grief or the Meaning of Life. He calls himself Mr E. F. Johnson. I can picture him already: old, cold, conventional, unwilling to talk about feelings. What sort of person puts "Mr" or "Mrs" in front of their own name nowadays?

I was brought up to believe that if you can't say anything nice you shouldn't say anything at all. I resent being done by as I would not do, but I cannot work out how to exact revenge. Then I wonder: do I know him? Maybe this is a pseudonym. Is he stupid, deranged even? (I'm over-reacting, I fear.)

In search of clues to Mr E. F. Johnson's identity and character, I spend half an hour studying his Amazon reviews. A surprise: seven five-star reviews for a classic nineteenth-century French novelist. I note with a warm feeling of superiority that he buys these books in English. No other books, except for a history of Northumberland. No modern novels except mine. Can he be a student, then? Reading French but not very good at it?

But no, not a student. There are indigestion pills and a cleaner for false teeth. All described as "very satisfactory". I bet he buys Viagra online too, but he doesn't review it. Best of all: a pair of pyjamas in olive green. He is delighted with the fit and the quality of the material. He likes the colour very much.

Mr E. F. Johnson has posted thirty-eight Amazon reviews. Two people have found his review of the pyjamas helpful.

I have him down as a sort of Pooterish character. Retired. Nothing better to do than write Amazon reviews and thinks his assessment of olive-green pyjamas will fascinate the wider public. So: someone whose opinions of my fine novel need not be taken too seriously. Not my "target reader."

\* \* \*

An unpleasant thought strikes me. What would someone infer about *me* from *my* Amazon customer reviews? Over a similar time period I have written about as many as Mr Johnson. I look them over. As well as some modern novels, I have reviewed a handful of nineteenth-century classics. And like Mr Johnson I have given all of them five stars. Mine too are French, and only one is *in* French.

Interspersed with the book reviews are the product reviews. Purchases I had long forgotten. Wooden clothes hangers. Five stars – how I loved them! And took the opportunity for a rant about the iniquity of making the things in plastic. Sounding like someone's pathetic old single auntie (which I am).

Toilet brushes and holders in black. Three stars. "Quite acceptable but unfortunately rather small and light, and easily knocked over."

And a nightie. Colour apricot. Brushed cotton. Five stars. "Very cosy and just the right length. Five stars well deserved."

I am beginning to think Mr E. F. Johnson and I may be kindred spirits after all. I wonder if he is married? He is. He reports that Mrs E. F. Johnson agreed with him about the indigestion pills and the false teeth cleaner. I hope she liked the pyjamas; he doesn't say. Maybe they have separate bedrooms. And I wonder if she is reading my novel. I expect he has told her not to.

The end


**How Many Stars?** was first published in *The Author,* Summer 2017, and reproduced in *The Oxford Writer,* spring, 2018. Revenge writing! Cleared by Society of Authors' lawyers.

# About the Author

Barbara Lorna Hudson grew up on a farm in Cornwall. She studied languages at Newnham College Cambridge and trained in social work at the Universities of Chicago and Newcastle. She was a psychiatric social worker and relationship counsellor for several years before becoming a social work lecturer, first at the London School of Economics and then at Oxford University.

When she retired, she took up fiction writing and completed the Guardian/University of East Anglia Certificate Course in Creative Writing.

Barbara began with short stories. Check out her e-book, *Click to Click: Tales of Internet Dating.* Her first novel *Timed Out* was published by Driven Press in 2016. *Timed Out* is about an older woman who tries to turn her life around via Internet dating, and looks for a meaningful way to spend her retirement years.

Barbara's first novel with Fantastic Books is *Makeover,* a story of tangled friendships and affairs that dips into the dark world of abusive relationships.

Barbara lives beside the Thames in Oxford, and spends a lot of time eating and talking at Green Templeton College, where she is an Emeritus Fellow.

Her website is www.barbaralornahudson.co.uk

If you have enjoyed this book, please consider leaving a review for Barbara Lorna Hudson to let her know what you thought of her work.

You can read about Barbara Lorna Hudson on her author page on the Fantastic Books Store. While you're there, why not browse our other delightful tales and wonderfully woven prose?

www.fantasticbooksstore.com